Cover Copy

To love and protect...across worlds.

The two warring nations on planet Magio have now been united under a leading team of eight—four warriors from Dralion and four protectors from Peacio—a team who must now work together to bring their divided nations back together as one.

Goldie Wincrest is a princess of Dralion, cursed with a skill she's never disclosed to another, an ability outlawed from their world centuries ago. She is a Chaser, one who must fight the deadly pull of her assassin ability, only she can no longer trust either herself or her fragmented thoughts any longer. There is only one pathway open to her, to choose her Destroyer and to give him the power he needs to see to her death should she go completely Dark.

Sorrell Sona is a fierce protector, a fighter of unparalleled strength, and when Goldie shares the knowledge of her outlawed ability with him, he is left in a terrible position. He must choose whether he can be her Destroyer should she become one of the Dark, or instead take a chance on seeking to be her savior.

Can he slay a princess of their world should she turn, or is he in too deep with her?

Books by Joanne Wadsworth

The Matheson Brothers Series
Highlander's Desire, Book One
Highlander's Passion, Book Two
Highlander's Seduction, Book Three
Highlander's Kiss, Book Four
Highlander's Heart, Book Five
Highlander's Sword, Book Six
Highlander's Bride, Book Seven
Highlander's Caress, Book Eight
Highlander's Touch, Book Nine
Highlander's Shifter, Book Ten
Highlander's Claim, Book Eleven
Highlander's Courage, Book Twelve
Highlander's Mermaid, Book Thirteen

Highlander Heat Series
Highlander's Castle, Book One
Highlander's Magic, Book Two
Highlander's Charm, Book Three
Highlander's Guardian, Book Four
Highlander's Faerie, Book Five
Highlander's Champion, Book Six
Highlander's Captive (Short Story)

Billionaire Bodyguards Series
Billionaire Bodyguard Attraction, Book One
Billionaire Bodyguard Boss, Book Two
Billionaire Bodyguard Fling, Book Three

Books by Joanne Wadsworth

Regency Brides Series
The Duke's Bride, Book One
The Earl's Bride, Book Two
The Wartime Bride, Book Three
The Earl's Secret Bride, Book Four
The Prince's Bride, Book Five
Her Pirate Prince, Book Six
Chased by the Corsair, Book Seven

Princesses of Myth Series
Protector, Book One
Warrior, Book Two
Hunter (Short Story - Included in Warrior, Book Two)
Enchanter, Book Three
Healer, Book Four
Chaser, Book Five

Chaser

Princesses of Myth, Book Five

Joanne Wadsworth

Chaser
ISBN-13: 978-1-99-003419-0
Copyright © 2017, Joanne Wadsworth
Cover Art by Joanne Wadsworth
First electronic publication: October 2017

Joanne Wadsworth
http://www.joannewadsworth.com

AUTHOR'S NOTE:
This book is a work of fiction. The names, characters, places, and incidents are products of the writer's imagination or have been used fictitiously and are not to be construed as real. Any resemblance to persons, living or dead, actual events, locale or organizations is entirely coincidental. The author does not have any control over and does not assume any responsibility for third-party websites or their content.

Published in the United States of America

First digital publication: October 2017
First print publication: September 2017

Chapter 1

"All I want to do is bleed a few protectors. What harm could possibly come of that?" I stood behind the wide trunk of an oak tree, a mere hundred feet from the protectors' battle-training arena.

"Goldie, we're not at war with the protectors of Peacio anymore." Hope Wincrest, my niece, who at eighteen was only a year younger than me, could talk sense into anyone, although right now I had no desire to listen to any form of sense.

"Don't turn on me now." We'd been raised together and were more like sisters who'd always had each other's backs. "At the very least, I should be able to raise my sword against the Peacian protectors in the name of training."

"Not when your desire isn't to train with them, but to slice and dice them."

"There's nothing wrong with a little slicing and dicing." I couldn't keep my grin from rising. Today, I'd awoken with the fierce need to vent some steam, and slicing and dicing would gleefully aid in that venting.

"I'm one of the leading eight of our world, charged with ensuring a peaceful transition now the energy dome over our country of Dralion is down." A huff as Hope planted her hands on her jean-clad hips, her outback shirt open at the collar with a bright red bandana tied in place at her neck.

"Spoilsport." I flicked the brim of Hope's Stetson, wishing I could flick her off instead since she wasn't being very helpful. "You should be rounding up the cattle. Our outback station won't run itself."

"You teleported me here with you, and Silas and Guy are currently looking after things in the outback."

"A lot of good it did bringing you along. You're trying to stifle my need to fight. I'm a warrior with the battle skill. Warriors need to release any pent-up tension by swinging their swords around, a dagger or two as well." I slid my wrist dagger free of its leather sheath and tossed it. It twirled through the air and landed smoothly in my palm. Once, twice, three times. Argh, I itched to toss it at a protector and see how quickly they could duck. I pushed off the tree and gave Hope my most determined look. "I'm going in. It's training time."

"No, you're not, not unless you promise not to kill any of them while undertaking this training." Hope blew out a long breath as she blocked my path, her blond hair whipping about in the breeze and her gaze narrowed, the deep violet of her eyes—the same shade as mine, which denoted our strong Wincrest bloodline—directed on me.

"Double spoilsport." I tweaked her chin. "Catch me if you can."

"Goldwyn Wincrest!" She yelled my name, but I'd already teleported and bumped down at the entrance of the arena a hundred feet distant, the iron gates raised high and her bellow carrying to me across the gravel and grass.

I pressed my hands to my hips, the short white sleeves of my shirt visible under my fitted black leather vest, the crisscross ties of my vest laced tight at the front to ensure I had no loose clothing these protectors could grab ahold of during a fight.

I slid my dagger back into my wrist sheath and strode determinedly inside. The open-aired arena, three-stories in height and of an ancient circular structure, was a beauty with its blocked seats layered back and up. It could hold thousands of spectators for when the Games began, the Games being the ancient tournament which brought together the most elite fighters for a battle of strength and will against each other.

"Hold up." Hope skidded in beside me. "You have to calm down and relax."

"There's no time for that." Wow. This protectors' arena was impressive, and extremely close in size to our warriors' arena in Dralion. I should have visited sooner now that the war had ended. In my hip-hugging black leather pants, I wandered around the inner circle of the safety barrier, my excitement rising for the training session to come.

On the central sandy floor, protectors trained in teams of two with swords and spears and battle axes in hand. The men wore battle leathers or red tunics with leather-flapped skirts, while the woman wore leather pants and vests similar to what I wore, all of them lunging and parrying as they fought with fiercely accurate strength, their weapons brutally sharp.

"If you're going to train with these protectors, then there must be rules." A huff from Hope.

"Rules, schmules."

"Stop giving me lip." She waved her hands in the air. "You aren't usually this combative. What's going on?"

"I'm sorry." I didn't mean to be so rude, not with her, but the urge to tangle with a protector grew stronger and stronger by the minute, and likely due to my raging new skill and the frustration of the dreams of foreboding hitting me once or twice a week, not that I could speak of those dratted dreams to anyone, especially not to Hope. Chaser. Ugh, that's what I now was, my infamous assassin ability outlawed centuries ago, the law governing it currently lying dormant since Chasers had been extinct for so long. That law would come flying back into being though, the second the news got out it had returned.

Heck, it had certainly shocked me when I'd fully

comprehended what had happened, and what I'd now become. Still, no matter the law, dormant or active, I needed to take all precautions and find myself a Destroyer. I certainly couldn't govern my own actions for the remainder of my days, not when Chasers eventually fought the deadly pull of their assassin ability, to the point when they could no longer trust either themselves or their fragmented thoughts any longer. My thoughts were headed that way. Fast.

At least I'd done my research.

I wanted a Destroyer from Peacio's Sona family line. The Sona bloodline was known to hold Destroyers within every generation, and brothers, Sorrell and Asar Sona, were at the top of my list. Either of them would be perfect for the job I required.

I needed both a guardian to keep me on the straight and narrow, then when I inevitably crossed the line of no return, for him to be my enforcer and ultimate destroyer. Maybe that wouldn't happen this week or this month, but it would happen sooner rather than later, and I needed to be prepared for when I went Dark.

Chasers certainly never remained on the loose for long, or even alive. Many in fact chose a Destroyer to see to their immediate death, rather than languishing in a steel-lined cell deep underground for the rest of their lives. Yep, and if I couldn't be riding across the great plains of Wincrest Station with Hope, then I'd rather end things completely. My choice. I patted the letter I'd written this morning in my inner shirt pocket, one which handed over the rights of my life to my Destroyer, with no recrimination to be sought against him once he'd been called to end my life.

The breeze lifted further, sweeping the sandy dust across the floor and blowing my long blond locks across my cheeks. Two sparring men of a colossal size, their faces grim and eyes blazing with retribution, fought in a supreme battle across the other side of the arena. They matched each other in height and they also fit the description of the Sona brothers which I'd taken firm note of.

Eagerness thrummed strongly through me as I gripped Hope's shoulder. I couldn't wait to come up against either of them. "I have a question."

"Shoot." She worried her bottom lip with her teeth.

"Would that be Sorrell and Asar Sona, by chance?" I pointed to the two men.

"Ah, y-yes." An uncertain answer, although not because she didn't know, but rather because she likely didn't want to confirm the truth with me, not when she understood my current feisty mood. Hope had spent a great deal of time on Peacian soil since her mate, Silas Carver, was both a protector and first cousin to Davio Loveria, Peacio's prince and future heir to King Carlisio Loveria's throne. This arena was Silas's playground and she'd watched her mate battle other protectors often during training sessions in this very place. "Why, in particular," she asked me, "are you after the Sona brothers?"

"They're fighters of unparalleled strength due to their destroyer ability."

She inhaled with a low whistle. "Why must you always go for the meanest sparring partners?"

"It's in my Wincrest blood to want to battle with the best of the best. Which Sona brother is which?" While undertaking my research, I'd discovered the brothers were twins, both born within two minutes of each other, Sorrell the eldest and the current leader of the mountain team of protectors, his younger twin, Asar, his second in command.

"The golden haired one is Sorrell, and the black haired one is Asar. Usually you can't tell the difference between them, but Asar recently dyed his hair black for a mission and the color hasn't yet washed out."

"Is it true those two don't show any emotion?"

"I've rarely seen any from them, but that's all due to their destroyer ability." A staying hand on my shoulder. "When the Sona brothers fight, they fight mean. That much I've definitely witnessed, so please, take all care when sparring with them."

"I will, and they sound perfect." I motioned to the safety barrier. Hope didn't hold the battle skill, so I needed her out of the way where she wouldn't get hurt. "How about you take a seat? I might be a while."

"If you cross any line in your training with them, then I'm breaking up the fight." She growled under her breath as she hugged me, then stepped back and bounded over the barrier. Elbows on the top edge, she leaned forward with a determined look, one all of us Wincrests had mastered.

I winked and faced the Sona brothers.

Time to meet my future Destroyer.

I brushed my sides and strode toward the two men as they swung at each other, their biceps bulging, chests broad and legs thick with muscles. The golden haired one struck with more aggression, his jaw clenched and eyes a steely-gray. Sorrell. Mmm, my kind of sparring partner. I wanted to go up against him first.

"Good morning, gentlemen." I slid my blade free of its scabbard, my heart and soul singing at having my weapon once again firm in my hand. My blade sang to me, the song a sweet tune which I completely adored. "I'd like to introduce myself. I'm—"

"I know who you are." Sorrell heaved away from Asar and sliced his sword in a vicious arc toward me. "You're Goldwyn Wincrest, a princess of Dralion, King Donaldo Wincrest's daughter."

"Call me Goldie. All my friends do."

"We're not friends." He rose to a towering height then he struck and our blades crashed dead center, the thunderous clang echoing across the floor. He pushed me back then heaved again and I met each of his hard strikes. Shouts and cheers abounded from the other training teams nearby.

"I hear you're the leader of the mountain team of protectors." Adrenaline pumped through my body, his form of brutal fighting calling strongly to the warrior within me, to the Chaser too.

"Correct. What of it?" His nostrils flared, his muscled chest rippling underneath the ripped strips of his almost non-existent white shirt. Even his pants weren't in one piece, the black leather worn here and there, across his knees and upper thighs, and as he twirled around following another harsh strike against me, I got a glimpse of both his lower butt cheeks through two slits.

"You've got a cute backside." I couldn't halt my teasing smile.

A curl of his lip. "I wore these pants to distract my bother during training, and it was working a real treat until you turned up."

"They're distracting me quite well." I angled my head and eyed him straight up. "If you like, I could even slice some more slits in that leather for you?"

"I'd like to see you try." He swung and came at me hard, again and again, landing several solid blows one after the other, then he twirled and attacked on my left side, each hit stronger than the last, no doubt in his attempt to see which sword hand I favored the most.

Luckily for me, I favored both my right and left equally, and two could play at his game. I switched my sword to the other hand and jabbed, managed to nick his ratty shirt. "Oooh, I'm getting closer to slicing those pants open, Sorrell."

"Why don't you zip your lips, Wincrest." A snort, his frustration clear to see.

"It's Goldie." I rocked from foot to foot, my knees loose and sword ready as he followed my every move. "You feel like going out for coffee after this session? I can sense the camaraderie growing between us. We could be great friends."

"I will never drink coffee with you." He snarled under his breath.

"You don't like coffee?"

"No, I prefer tea, in a fine bone china cup, with a matching saucer."

"Haha." I laughed, a giggle escaping me. "So, you really don't wanna do coffee?"

"No. Nada. Zilch. Never." He swung and I caught his next two teeth-jarring hits and managed to slam one back at him. "You got that, or do I need to spell it out, Princess?"

"I told you, it's Goldie." Although I quite liked how *Princess* rolled off his tongue, all husky and hard. "Haven't you heard that it's important to know your opponent?"

"Of course." He kicked up dust as he swung with another teeth-jarring hit. "Do you prefer your coffee white or black?"

"Black, with three teaspoons of sugar." I whipped around, my blade slicing the leather of his pants, right across the low waistline. "How do you like your tea?"

"With blood in it." Jaw clenched, he circled me. "Have you got any you'd like to spill?"

"Nope, although I'd like to see you try and spill some. I believe you're all talk and no action."

"Don't tempt me." His gaze drilled into mine, his fist flexing over his sword hilt.

"It's a pain, right? This current peace agreement between our countries?"

"It is for those of us who have always enjoyed a decent fight with your country's warriors." He heaved forward, his blow knocking me back onto my backside and sand flying as I skidded across the floor.

Whoa, I hadn't expected that hit, which had been twice the force of his last ones.

I scrambled to get back onto my feet, but he swung again and I barely grappled to meet his attack, our blades crashing a mere inch from my nose. My arms shook as I clasped the hilt and tried to rise, although Sorrell pushed down harder, his blade drawing closer toward my neck. Good grief. Should I breathe too deep, I would certainly feel the cold steel of his blade slicing into my throat.

"Do you admit defeat?" he muttered, his nose almost touching my nose, his spicy, leathery aroma floating tantalizingly around me.

"Even if I do, don't take your gaze off me."

"Duly noted." He remained right where he was, his gaze and hold steady. "As much as I'd love to kill you, unfortunately, I might hang for it. Put your weapon down and I'll step back."

"You're not fighting King Donaldo's daughter right now, you're fighting a warrior who wouldn't hesitate to spill your blood if I could." I dropped my sword and heaved to the side. He lost his balance, and I kicked his shin as I rolled free, his blade almost nicking my ear as he caught onto my shenanigans.

"Sorrell, if you put even one scratch on Goldie, I'm going to be very angry with you." Hope jumped the barrier and bore down on us.

"I'm fine," I shot back at her as I nabbed my sword, then barely ducked Sorrell's next blow. Air whistled right past my neck. "You fight like a girl," I hissed at him, hoping like crazy I could keep pushing his buttons. "You're a Destroyer. Start destroying."

"If I allowed my full strength to rise against you, you'd be dead already." He slid his blade back into his scabbard, his heavily muscled chest rising and falling as he sent me a daggered look with eyes not entirely a steely-gray as I'd first thought, but actually holding a hint of soft blue at the edge. With his golden hair, all shaggy and brushing his shoulders, he appeared like an Adonis of old. Strikingly gorgeous, that's if one could call a heavily muscled protector gorgeous.

"At least I made you work hard during that session." Yep,

he was the Destroyer I wanted. He'd be absolutely perfect at keeping me in line. I shoved out a hand, hoping he'd take the bait and end our session on a professional note, and I couldn't keep my smile at bay as he gritted his teeth and slapped his hand against mine.

Double perfect.

I gripped his fingers tightly, then 'ported and sent us shimmering away through space and time, directly to my own backyard in the outback, or at least close enough. We bumped down underneath the wide boughs of an oak tree next to the river bordering Wincrest Station, this the only spot on our land where the grass actually grew due to the controlled river releases we used to flood these lower fields. Beyond the grass lay thousands of hectares of dry red dust, the current drought killing our land.

"Why the hell did you bring me here?" He searched about. "This is Wincrest Station in the outback, right?"

"Yes. I needed to speak to you in private, and this is the place I've chosen."

"If you actually need to speak to me, then you'll do so within my own territory. Allow me." He grasped my arms and sent us zipping back through the same tunnel of darkness, stars zooming past.

I thudded down on a crunchy matting of fallen leaves and pine nettles and almost lost my balance as Sorrell released me. I wobbled at the edge of a sheer cliff where it fell away with rolling forested hills spread out far into the distance. A thick layer of gray cloud swept across the sky, from horizon to horizon.

A storm brewed, and not just within nature, but within the man at my back too.

I righted myself and went to turn around, only I changed my mind.

I stayed exactly where I was.

"You're giving me your back, Princess. You do realize that,

right?" His deep voice floated over me as he loomed from behind, his intoxicating aroma as well.

"That's because I already trust you." I would be prickling with unease otherwise.

"Like hell you do." A snort, his disbelief clear to hear.

"Honestly, I do." The tips of my boots rode the fine edge of the cliff where the odd leaf whisked away in the breeze and fluttered over the steep side. Slowly, I turned around and faced him, my gaze directly on his. "Do you want to know how and why?"

"Sure, explain yourself, because right now I'm incredibly tempted to toss you over this cliff."

"I have a very new and extremely aggravating skill." I dipped my head, closed my eyes and braced myself for the truth I now needed to speak. "One day soon," I continued as I lifted my gaze back to his, "I will need you to see to my death."

"Well, today works for me." Seizing my arms, he tipped me back until I leaned right over the edge of the ledge at a rather precarious angle, my blond hair fluttering and my sword swaying back heavily on my hip.

I didn't fight his move though, one which showed his clear dominance, which was exactly what had brought me to him in the first place. "You speak my kind of language, Sorrell."

His brow shot into his hairline.

Then a grunt as he hauled me back in and let go.

He pointed through the dense line of the trees. "The barracks and log cabins of my mountain team are about a hundred feet in. We can speak there."

"How many protectors?"

"The number varies."

"Twenty? Fifty? A hundred?" I needed to know what to expect.

"About that." He crossed his arms, his feet planted wide, his answer no help at all.

"Goldie?" Hope's voice rebounded inside my head. *"You okay?"*

"Yep, I just wanted to chat to Sorrell. I'm not sure how long I'll be. Getting information out of him right now is like pulling teeth."

"What kind of information are you trying to uncover?"

"If he's dating anyone."

"Ha, sure you are."

"I like him."

"You do not."

"Do too." I wasn't even lying. For some reason, I truly did like the big, beefy fighter in front of me. Even the rips in his clothing held a certain appeal. *"Can you make your own way back to the outback? I might be a little while."*

"Silas is here, so I'm gonna catch a ride home with him, and you can be sure I'll be after more information about you and Sorrell when you return. No ducking and diving around the issue either. Be careful, okay?"

"I'll be on my best behavior." I closed our link before she got even more inquisitive, planted my own feet wide and crossed my arms, matching my adversary as well as I could.

"Who were you speaking to?" Narrowed eyes, yet feisty, sexy narrowed eyes.

"Hope. She was checking in, as she likes to do with me from time to time. Silas is taking her back to the station, so that way you and I can chat for as long as we like."

"I'd rather not chat at all." He cocked his head to one side. "Are you and Silas close?"

"Yes, although far too close for my comfort." A snarky answer, but hey, it was the truth. I'd had to accept Silas Carver being around, particularly since he'd forged a mated bond with Hope, the two soon to be wed. I also couldn't deny how much he loved Hope, which in my eyes was his most redeeming quality.

"What about Davio Loveria? My prince is mated to Hope's

twin sister, Faith. Are you close with Davio at all?" He tapped one booted foot.

"We're learning to tolerate each other." My Wincrest blood surged forth whenever I was within five feet of Davio or any of his Loveria family. Such an uncomfortable feeling, like needles being stabbed into my skin, but yeah, apart from that and because of Faith, he was now family and I'd had to accept that.

"For some reason"—he frowned something fierce, which was huge since he'd already been frowning fiercely—"I can actually sense the truth when you speak it. Strange."

"Well, I haven't lied to you yet, and I don't intend to either." For him to be my Destroyer, immense trust would be needed between us, particularly when I'd be placing my life, and coming death, in his hands. I tugged the inside of my shirt collar and cleared my throat. "Is there somewhere we can speak where we can't be overheard? Our voices could travel easily from this cliff face."

"I have a log cabin close, just along from my men's barracks. No one will disturb us there. You've also intrigued me, particularly since you said you need me to see to your death. Come with me." He marched away, his shoulders broad and peeks of his bronze skin showing through the rips in his shirt. Along a trail weaving through the dense line of pines, he strode.

Breathing deep, I followed and took in the heady pine freshness of the forest and the heavy richness of the soil underfoot. Mushrooms poked through the underbrush near the base of the trees I passed, the heads so large they'd cover my entire dinner plate if I served them up for a meal.

As I came alongside a particularly thick patch of green grass, I couldn't help but stop and clutch a handful. I pressed the lush blades against my nose, the stalks as soft as velvet.

"What are you doing?" A grating question where he'd halted a few steps ahead, his gaze speculative. "Is something wrong?"

"Nope. I simply love grass—looking at it, holding it, and smelling it." I stuffed the grass into the pocket of my black leather pants. This would be a wonderful treat for one of my station's horses when I returned home. "Don't you?"

"Not enough to want to carry it on me."

"You've no idea how lucky—" A fat drop splashed my cheek and I glanced up at the leafy foliage overhead, the odd gap showing the stormy clouds I'd noted before. "Is it going to rain right now?"

"Yeah, and when it rains in these hills, we get a downpour. We've no time to stand around waiting for that to happen, otherwise we'll get soaked." He gripped my hand and dragged me through the trees.

"Getting soaked sounds amazing." Another drop splashed my nose and I tried to yank my hand out of his, only he tightened his grip, so I gritted my teeth and growled as I got hauled toward his cabin, my booted feet skidding in the grass. "You are a very mean protector."

"We're almost there." Grinning, and far too smugly for my liking, he powered on.

"I really want to kill you."

"Not happening, not on my watch." He pulled me out of the trees and into a large clearing with log-built barracks and cabins sprinkled about.

A central fire blazed in a wide pit with logs pulled up around it for seating. A pig pushed its snout into a feed trough and guzzled the scraps within. No other protectors about. All remained completely quiet, other than for the rowdy swine. "Who does the pig belong to?"

"That's Zachariah. He has free run of the place, but don't get on his bad side, or he'll annoy the hell out of you."

"Like what you're doing with me right now?"

"Pretty much."

"Where are your team?"

"They'll all be out on assignment, due back at the change of shift in another twenty minutes, which is when I'm due on duty. I can give you twenty minutes and no more." He strode toward the log cabin farthest from the others, a little out on its own where a river weaved through the woods behind it.

How beautiful, and quaint. Such a dreamy spot.

With a front porch and an overhanging roof of wooden shingles, his cabin appeared rustic and quite charming. "Slow down. I want to take everything in." I tugged and tried to free my hand again, and this time managed to. "That's better."

"Inside now." He pushed open the front door and gestured for me to enter.

"This isn't going to be fun." I groaned and grumped as I stomped inside.

"For me either." He shut the door, jabbed a finger at the small side table with two wooden-backed chairs next to it. "Sit."

"Yes, sir." I scraped out a chair and eased into it. Out the window beside me, rain splattered the river and the heavy boughs of the trees. A large bird with blue feathers hopped across an overhanging ledge of rocks, river water streaming over it. It dipped its beak into the water, drank then with a flap of its winged feathers, flicked water over itself.

I pulled my gaze from the playful bird and checked over my shoulder. A bathroom was visible through an open door at the end of his cabin, and against two of the four log walls, two single beds sat covered in thickly quilted covers. Across every inch of his walls, a variety of weaponry hung—large shields, swords of different lengths and styles, a couple of war hammers, and half a dozen battle axes. My kind of weaponry collection. "I like the décor."

"Don't touch any of it, or I'll slice your fingers off."

"You remind me of my childhood tutor. He used to be as brisk and mean as you." He'd retired after tutoring me, but he'd constantly reprimanded me for not sitting still, usually because I preferred being outside rather than confined to the tutoring room. At least I'd had Hope with me during those schooling years, which had helped ease the tediousness of it all. She and I would whisper and giggle, as well as play tricks on the elderly man. Mischief-makers, he'd called us, and we still were. I crossed my legs and motioned to the other chair. "Would you care to join me?"

"Start talking." He plucked a bottle of water from a shelf next to a tall dresser and tossed it to me before taking his seat. With his booted feet kicked out and his gaze pinpointed on me, he appeared both relaxed and coiled with tension.

"Long story short." Best I give him the news that way. I unscrewed the lid, gulped a mouthful of water and set the bottle down with a *thump*. "I'm a Chaser."

"I wasn't born yesterday, Princess." He tapped the tabletop. "Chasers have been extinct for centuries, and my kind put them into that extinction."

"Honestly, I am, and I've no reason to lie to you." I waited and waited as he simply stared at me. I blew out a long breath. "Okay, I'm absolutely telling you the truth, and I need you to be my Destroyer. Think about it, why would I even come to you about such a deathly matter and mention it, if it weren't true?"

"There aren't even any families with the assassin skill surviving. If you do have it, then how'd you come by it?"

Okay, I was getting somewhere. Questions were good.

"It's not a skill that's ever run through my Wincrest family line, or at least not until now. I'm the first, and I'll also be the last since I've no intention of passing my ability on to any children I might bear. It's the only responsible thing to do, to cut the Chaser line off here and now with me."

"A wise decision."

"Do you believe me?"

"You're right. It is a deathly matter and there's no reason for you to mention it unless you truly were a Chaser." He nabbed my bottle and swigged a mouthful. "Are you mated?"

"If I am, my mate has never come for me." Which would mean, when it came time for him to end my life, he would have no overprotector mate fighting him for my survival. "I'm alone, and will remain alone. I give you my word I will."

"Why'd you choose me?" He leaned forward, elbows to the table.

"You're from Peacio's strongest line of Destroyers. Why wouldn't I choose you?"

"You're Donaldo's daughter. Why haven't you chosen a Destroyer from Dralion?"

"I can't trust one of my own countrymen to slay me, not due to who I am. With you, who I am is an incentive to issue that death strike." I propped my elbows on the table too. If I leaned forward, I could easily reach out and touch him. "I need you to agree to my request, and I'll do whatever it takes to obtain it. For starters, you have my permission to end my life in whatever way you wish. I won't fight your choice of death kill, or the time of that death, provided you're certain I've crossed the line of no return."

"I'm starting to warm up to the idea of saying yes." A glint sparked in his eyes. "Keep going. Give me some more incentive."

"They say you're without emotions, your brother too."

"All Destroyers are. What of it?"

"Burdening my loved ones with my new ability isn't an option, so all I ask is that you don't say a word to them. Other than that, I'm at your disposal. If you wish, you can use me to elevate your own standing within your country. Even though Dralion and Peacio are no longer at war, there are still pockets of hatred which simmer here and there between our countrymen. One can't end a thousand-year-old war and expect there to be roses the next day. You'd be the protector who took down Donaldo Wincrest's daughter, with no retaliation to bear upon you. You'd be a legend in your own right."

"I have no desire to be a legend."

"Okay, then you'd be doing both your country and mine a huge favor by agreeing to my request. Chasers were outlawed for a reason, and no one wants them back." My chest tightened, pain lancing through me. The thought of leaving my family, of causing them any hurt or heartache, ripped my own heart in two.

"You're right. No one wants the Chasers back." He picked up a pen and pad from the table and slid both across to me. "To accept the position of your Destroyer, I need a signed letter stating that should you perish at my hand, that I had your complete and utter permission to instigate that slaying."

"I've already written a letter." I plucked the envelope containing it from my shirt pocket and handed it to him. "All I need to do is add your name."

He read the letter and handed it back. "Sorrell S. Sona."

I fiddled with the pen, scrawling in a small circle at the corner of the letter until the ink came down. I wrote his name in. "What's the middle *S* stand for?"

"Saber."

"Oh, nice. It suits you."

"Are you done? I have a shift, remember?"

"Sorry." After a deep breath, I folded the letter and tucked it back inside the envelope. I pushed it across to him, the pad and pen too.

"Are you suffering from the dreams of foreboding yet?" He wrote "personal" across the front of the envelope then tucked it next to a pile of papers to one side of the table.

"Yes, but they're only hitting once or twice a week, the same dream, and so far, the two people within it, the victim and the murderer, aren't clear enough to be seen."

"Tell me more about the dream."

"There's a rocky hillside with trees lit silver by the moonlight, two men scaling it. A bitter fight breaks out near the plateau, and well, it's clear murder takes place. Quite calculated by the killer."

"You haven't tried to locate the rocky hillside?"

"It could be any hillside." I'd also awoken from those dreams drenched in sweat and a sense of impending doom and failure searing through me, more so last night than ever before. "I'm too late as well."

"What do you mean?"

"One identifying marker within the dream became clear—the day and time the murder occurred, by last night's full moon."

"Unfortunately, that's the way of a Chaser's dreams at times."

"I fear the next dream that arises."

"I'll maintain a tight watch over you."

"How?"

"I'll need all the 'porting images for the places you can usually be found, including your bedroom. You have any issue with that?"

"Nope."

"All Chasers are driven by the urge to track down the guilty party they've seen in their dreams, whether that guilty party is actually guilty of the crime you've witnessed within your dreams or not."

"I'm aware. Chasers soon become little more than killing machines, taking on the role of the judge, jury, and executioner, all in one. Or at least until their Destroyer locks them away." I searched his gaze. "Sorrell, I don't want to be locked away, have already chosen death over captivity. Can you make certain that happens?"

"Absolutely. That'll be my pleasure." He tapped his head. "You said you trust me. Show me your trust by forging the telepathic link of trust between us."

"Of course." I reached out with my telepathic skill and forged a path directly to his mind. I connected with ease, my trust in him absolute, or at least my trust in him now carrying out his duty to me. Mind to mind, I muttered, *"I've done my homework. You're a Sona, born to a strong line of fierce Destroyers, a man who will carry out his duty once your oath is given."*

A slow nod. "Why are you keeping your family in the dark?"

"Would you tell your family you were a Chaser, if you discovered that to be the truth?"

"Destroyer lines have never blended with Chaser lines, so that's an impossibility." He pushed his chair back and stood. "Let's complete our agreement so I can meet my men, and by the way, you have my respect for coming to me."

"Bet you never thought you'd say that to a Wincrest."

"You'd win that bet for sure." A slow smile lifted his lips and with a dip of his head, he removed his dagger and sliced his palm. "I offer you a blood oath, Princess."

"I accept." I cut my own palm with my dagger and shook his hand. "When do you want to collect those 'porting images of all my regular haunts?"

"Later today when I'm off duty, or tomorrow. I'll be in touch." He strode out the door and clicked it shut behind him, which was a surprise.

He'd left me alone in his quarters.

I turned my hand over and traced the pink line of my palm as the skin sealed, my fast-healing ability ensuring the injury mended swiftly. I should leave too, only I was in my Destroyer's cabin and I wouldn't mind getting to know him better.

Hmm, the nosy warrior within me was already wandering about.

All remained clean and tidy, no clothes dropped on the floor or half poking out of his dresser drawers. In fact, he kept his room utilitarian clean, without any personal—wait, a book. Definitely a personal item.

I crossed to his nightstand and picked up the book. The cover showed a road of red dust leading to one of the more famous rocks in the outback.

Oh, the outback.

Interesting.

The title displayed *Expeditions into the Scorching Heat of the Outback.*

Double interesting.

He was keen on learning more about my backyard. He hadn't mentioned that when I'd first zipped us there.

I flipped the book open to the spot where a bookmark poked out.

Nope, not quite a bookmark, but a photo with crinkled edges, a photo showcasing a watering hole surrounded by boulders on one side and the dusty red plains of the outback on the other. It could be one of any thousands of watering holes found in the outback, only this one was incredibly familiar. It sat on Wincrest Station, the closest watering hole to my homestead.

I turned the photo over and arched a brow at the date penciled across the back. *August twenty-ninth.* No year mentioned, but that date matched my birthday.

Hmm, triple interesting, and how on earth had he gotten this?

I reached out to Hope, hoping she might have an answer. *"Hey, I have a question. It's about Sorrell."*

"Shoot."

"I'm at Sorrell's cabin and he's left for a shift. I should have left too, but I got nosy and now I've found a book about the outback on his nightstand with a photo tucked inside, one showcasing the watering hole closest to our station. It's got the date of August twenty-ninth penciled on the back, which of course is the date of my birthday. That's raising all sorts of questions in my mind."

"Oh, I have the answer to that. Sorrell actually made a trip

out here with Silas a week ago. You'd been called to a meeting with Donaldo in Dralion and missed his visit. Sorrell is within Davio and Silas's inner circle and needed to store the teleporting images of the places where they pop by when in the outback. A security measure. After Silas and I showed him around the homestead, we took him into town where he picked up a book and purchased some other knickknacks. We dropped by a couple of the watering holes since he seemed keen to look around, and he took a couple of pictures. After that, he headed back for a shift. Sorry, I should have mentioned it."

"No, that's okay, and thanks for answering my question." Davio and Silas had brought a few of their most trusted protectors through the station to ensure they had the teleporting images, so Hope's answer definitely explained this book and photo, only why had Sorrell written August twenty-ninth on the back? What a secretive man. After a quick goodbye, I closed my link with her then tapped at Sorrell's mind. *"Hey, long time no talk."*

"What do you want, Princess?"

"I've been snooping about your cabin."

"Somehow, I'm not surprised. Did you find anything of interest?"

"Yes, a book on your nightstand about the outback, along with a photo of the watering hole closest to my homestead. Hope told me you paid a visit to my home a week ago. Why didn't you tell me?"

"That visit meant nothing."

"It meant enough for you to purchase souvenirs from in town. Why pencil the date of August twenty-ninth on the back? That's my birthday."

"I wasn't aware." His bored tone echoed back at me. *"Are we done with this conversation yet?"*

"No. Does that date mean something special to you?"

"Nope."

"C'mon, spill." Good grief. Trying to get information out of him was like trying to wring water from a rock.

"I'm your Destroyer, not your buddy who spills his heart out."

He shut the link with a swift snap.

I tried to reopen it, only I hit a block wall.

Grrr, he'd blocked me.

How incredibly annoying.

Chapter 2

Hours later, frustration still hummed through me as I mucked out the stalls and fed the breeding mares. Another two tasks done for the day, with plenty more still to go even though the sun had already begun its descent toward the horizon. I slid my black leather vest off and hung it from a hook inside the main holding room of the stables, then nabbed my Stetson from the next hook and settled it on my head. I leaned against the splintered edge of the doorway and eyed the red plains that ran forever into the distance.

Even with sunset so close, scorching heat still rose from the dusty ground like tendrils of swirling vapor. Outside in the high-railed wooden corral, Guy Moyer, a warrior who held the ability to enchant through spells he spoke, held the reins of a gelding he'd recently trained to take a saddle on his back. Now he rode in that saddle, the horse taking his weight superbly. Guy was an excellent horseman and trainer and had earned my respect. I trusted him implicitly, just as I trusted Hope and Faith.

I pushed off the doorway, strode to the corral then climbed the high wooden beams and perched on the uppermost one. With my legs swinging down one side, I tucked one loose white shirttail into my hip-hugging black leather pants. "One day it's going to rain, and when it does, I'm going to shout and roll around in the fields like a lunatic."

"I'll be shouting and rolling around with you." He gave me a quirky grin as he trotted around the perimeter of the corral, the gelding holding a fluid gait. "It's a shame Maslin is away visiting his grandparents in No-Man's Land. He wanted to be here when I completed this horse's training. Are you still thinking about giving this horse to Saunder as a gift?"

"Absolutely. Saunder's fourteenth birthday is only a week away, and Star Shine has a dependable nature and will be perfect for him." Saunder—the young son of warrior Tawson Rivera—had lived with us following his father's capture during the war, but with the war now over and Tawson returned to us, both father and son now resided here in the barracks together and were a treasure to have around. "When will Star Shine's training be complete?"

"Within the week."

"Did I hear someone say gift?" With his messy brown hair flopping forward over his brow, Saunder beamed as he bounced across the yard, his suspenders barely holding up his loose, long-legged tan pants. "Is Star Shine really gonna be mine?"

"Yes, big ears, as soon as Guy has completed his training, which I bet you heard would be done within the week." Laughing, I patted the rail beside me. "Haul yourself up here, squirt."

"Thank you, thank you, thank you," he gushed as he clambered up the rails.

"You're welcome, and every warrior-in-training needs their own mount." I pulled Saunder into a squishy hug, the lad most definitely in training, a future warrior in the making. "Have you finished your schoolwork for the day?" His tutor 'ported in from Dralion five afternoons a week and he attended sessions in my old tutoring room on the lower floor of the homestead.

"Yep, all done. I learnt all about heat conduction and transfer by c-convection today," he stammered a little, the unfamiliar word one he clearly hadn't heard before.

"Did it make any sense?" I'd hated that topic during my schooling years.

"Well, my tutor told me the Earth's surface is warmed by the sun, then when the warm air rises, cooler air moves in. Except that doesn't seem to happen here, so not much sense. It's never cool in the outback."

"It's a little cooler at night." Only by a few degrees, a miniscule amount, but it made enough of a difference so that one could sleep without dripping in sweat. I bumped my shoulder into Saunder's. "Do you want to go for a ride with me to Gullaroo field? After a tough tutoring session, the best thing to do is to sneak out for a ride."

"I'd love to." He jiggled about, eagerness brightening his eyes.

"Great. The water barrels at Gullaroo need checking. We'll see to that chore while we're there."

"I'll saddle two horses." He bounded down and sprinted toward the stables. There was never any holding Saunder back from a ride across the plains, me either.

"You two are like two peas in a pod." Guy slowed to a trot and dismounted with a *thump* on the hard ground, the red dust rising over his boots and the lower hem of his jeans. Our resident warrior enchanter righted his Stetson, his midnight-black hair poking out from underneath. "I'm glad, particularly since he doesn't have a mother and needs a woman's influence in his life."

"I hate that he lost his mother so young. He didn't get the chance to know her." The same had happened to me, unfortunately. My mother had passed away following my birth, and I'd always been able to relate to Saunder in that way.

"Hey, you two." With her bright red bandana a splash of vivid color at her neck, Hope strolled toward me along the dusty pathway leading from the homestead, a towering stand of eucalyptus trees to the side and Silas one step behind her as he clicked the gate shut. Hope climbed the railing and sat on the beam next to me. With a pat of my leg, she arched a brow. "Right," she muttered. "Give me the run down on everything that happened between you and Sorrell, and don't leave anything out. Not one thing."

"Yeah, I'd like to know all about you and Sorrell too." Silas, his billowy blue shirt flapping loose over his black jeans, leaned against the railing, one booted foot wedged on the lower beam, his arms crossed over the top rail. "Last week Sorrell was keen to drop by here for the 'porting locations where Davio and I can be found. Hope and I showed him around, and now this week you two are hanging out. Why the sudden interest in one of my fellow protectors?"

"I wanted a new sparring partner."

"There's more to it than that." A squeeze of my leg from Hope.

"Aren't we supposed to be getting along with our ex-enemy now? Or at least trying to?"

"Yes, but—"

"Maybe I like him, Hope." I had to sidetrack her questioning fast, Silas's too. "Sorrell knows how to wield his sword and is dedicated to his mountain team. I admire both those attributes in him, and in the future, he'll be popping by from time to time for more training sessions with me." I struck a look at Guy, who was staring at me like I was an alien. I huffed and muttered at him, "C'mon, you're much worse than me at hanging around protectors. You're mated to Silvie, a protector with the fire skill, and honestly, I'm feeling a little left out so I'm trying to make some protector friends myself."

I barely kept a straight face as I said that. These days, I was surrounded by more protectors than I cared for, but I could handle them, provided I had some warriors within the mix too.

"Ooo-kay," Hope murmured.

"Sorrell would make a fierce sparring partner for her." Silas hooked his hands around Hope's jean-clad hips, his gaze on his mate. "That's definitely true and makes sense."

"I guess." Hope settled one arm around Silas's neck as she leaned back against him.

"Yeah, I agree. Sorrell is the toughest protector to spar with. I've gone a couple of rounds against him." Guy plucked a treat from his pocket and offered it to the gelding, then snuck a brush from the top of the post and gently rubbed the horse down. "He doesn't show a lot of emotions though, just slams his blade right into you."

"I like that he keeps his emotions to himself." The truth, and he'd better make sure he always kept those emotions to himself. I certainly didn't want a guardian and Destroyer who cared about me. All I needed him to do was maintain his end of our bargain, to be my guardian with a watchful eye, my enforcer to ensure I kept to the straight and narrow, and in the end, once I'd crossed the line of no return, my ultimate destroyer.

Star Shine lifted his sleek head and pushed his muzzle into my leg. He snorted and sniffed, then pushed higher, right over my hip pocket where a few blades of grass waved free. Grinning, I pulled out the wad I'd nabbed from the mountains this morning and scratched between the gelding's silky ears. Snout butting into my palm, he gobbled the grass.

Hope patted the gelding's neck, then tapped her head. "It's Faith 'pathing me." She went quiet for a minute before smiling wide. "She and Davio are on their way. Apparently, Sorrell is with them."

"Really?" I reached out and touched my mind to Sorrell's. *"Are you off duty already?"*

"I wasn't, but Davio collected me from the mountains after hearing about our training session. I got quizzed about it. It seems nothing escapes my prince for long."

"What did you tell him?"

"That you're strong and fierce on the training floor, that I

found your wily underhanded tricks entertaining."

"*I told everyone here I needed a new sparring partner.*"

"*Okay, we'll go with that.*"

The air swirled and Davio Loveria shimmered in with Faith nestled in front of him, Sorrell at his back, my Destroyer's shaggy blond hair flying back from his shoulders and his determined gaze zeroing in on me.

I gave my new sparring partner a wink. "Welcome to Wincrest Station. I wish I'd been here the first time you visited."

"Thanks." A grunt as he surveyed the area, taking in the sprawling homestead on the hill built in earth-toned bricks. Three floors high and with a wide wraparound porch, it held darkened glass windows which kept the harshest of the sun's rays at bay.

"Are you all right after that 'port? You seem quiet." Davio turned Faith by the shoulders to face him, his billowy white shirt donned under a tan leather vest, his daggers sheathed at both wrists and sword hooked at his hip over dark pants. Peacio's prince never went anywhere unarmed, just as his protectors didn't.

"I'm perfectly fine. I might be pregnant, but I'm as strong as ever. I do hold the battle skill, remember?" With her violet eyes sparking, Faith reached up on her sneakered toes and hooked her arms around his neck, her white top swaying over the belted waist of her denim shorts, the slight rise of her belly showing. A multitude of daggers glinted, one strapped to her wrist, another to her ankle, while a third poked out from the small of her back where she'd slotted it into her shorts. "I'm super hungry though and haven't eaten since lunchtime. That's why I'm quiet. I'd kill for some food."

"For real food or for some of your bizarre pregnancy craving food?" Davio dipped her back, his dark brown hair wisped with a golden-brown sweeping forward as he pressed a kiss to the tip of her nose.

"What exactly do you call bizarre?"

"Those spicy, red-hot peppers you have a constant craving for."

"Peppers aren't bizarre, but I'm not actually craving peppers right now." She tapped his chin. "I'm craving frozen bananas, big-time, and I don't mean banana flavored ice cream. I mean actual bananas, peeled, then frozen whole, served with ice cream on the side."

"That doesn't sound too bad. I could go for some of that." He righted Faith back on her feet.

"I know the perfect ice cream parlor in New Zealand that sells what I'm after, and it's right near my old high school. You up for a quick trip?"

"Always." He lifted a brow at Sorrell. "I'll catch up with you later. Enjoy your visit here."

A nod from Sorrell.

"Wait up. We're coming too. Those frozen bananas and ice cream sound yum." Hope jumped down from the rail and grasped ahold of Faith's hand, Silas swinging in behind her. The two girls, both born together, were identical in every way, and thankfully they'd also forged a strong bond since being reunited after so many years apart. It was wonderful to see them together, to know they had each other once more.

"Great. Let's go." Davio shimmered and disappeared with Faith, Hope and Silas flashing away with them.

I bounded down from the rail and moseyed on over to Sorrell. "If you've got time, I'm riding out to Gullaroo field with Saunder. We need to check the level of the water barrels. Would you like to come?" It'd give me the chance to show him around, perhaps to places he hadn't seen during his first trip here.

"Who's Saunder?" He glanced at Guy over my head and lifted his chin in acknowledgement of him.

"Saunder's the son of one of our warriors here at the station." I stuffed two fingers between my lips and went to whistle, only I stopped as Saunder led two saddled horses out of the stables. "You've got perfect timing."

I accepted the reins of both mounts and handed one set of reins to Sorrell. I bounded into the saddle of my stallion and extended a hand to Saunder. No time for him to saddle a third mount, not when Saunder could ride just as easily with me, and not when the sun would be setting soon enough. I tugged Saunder up behind me and offered introductions. "Saunder, meet Sorrell Sona, a protector from Peacio. He's joining us. Late notice. Sorry about that."

"Hi ya." Saunder offered him a cheerful smile. "Nice to meet you."

I nudged my stallion closer to Sorrell as he mounted. "Sorrell, meet Saunder, my favorite thirteen-year-old in the entire world."

"Hey, kid." Sorrell jerked his head toward the plains where a massive red rock sat underneath the vivid blue of the outback sky. "Lead the way, Princess. I'm eager to see more of your outback."

"Try to keep up, if you can. We ride hard and fast in the outback." I shoved my knees into my stallion's flanks and with Saunder holding on tight from behind, I grinned and gave my horse his head.

"I'll keep up," he yelled from behind.

I flew out of the yard, my shirttails flapping and adrenaline pumping.

Across the field scattered with a few stalks of dry grass, I tore, dust streaming in my wake.

Sorrell galloped in alongside us, a crooked smile lifting his lips and his ripped white t-shirt plastered against his chest.

Beaming and lifting his face into the wind, Saunder had one scrawny arm wrapped around my waist, his other planted on the rear hump of the saddle to keep him seated. "Can we 'port, Goldie?"

"We sure can." I tucked myself in closer to my stallion's neck and rode low and fast, and once Saunder leaned into my back and did the same, I 'ported, without any warning to Sorrell. He'd be able to keep up, hopefully.

I made the swift leap through time and space directly to Gullaroo field, galloping smoothly from one dusty plain to another, the blast of added speed from my stallion making my pulse race.

Following our 'porting airstream, Sorrell joined us in a rush of wind, his horse's hooves pounding the hard ground.

Up ahead, the familiar cluster of bush trees bordering the dried-out watering hole of Gullaroo came into view and I slowed. Moving into a trot, I patted my mount's silky neck then halted beside the first of the water barrels.

I dismounted, Saunder jumping down too, the lad taking the reins and hooking them to the hitching post where the horse could easily reach the barrel for a drink.

Sorrell looped his reins to the same post and joined me. "Do you want those barrels checked first?"

"Yep, before it gets dark. You head left and I'll head right. Each barrel needs checking, so don't miss any out."

"Will do." He strode away.

Our two horses dunked their snouts into the water with throaty snickers, each splashing the other before lifting their heads and playfully butting their muzzles together.

I nabbed a bottle of water from the saddlebags and tossed it to Saunder. "Stay hydrated."

"Can I explore?" He motioned to the trees.

"Absolutely, but yell out if you need me." The cows often sought coverage from the sun within those trees, which was where I wouldn't mind being at the moment. I got to work, taking the right and swinging around each barrel on my way around the dried basin of the watering hole. Half of them were drained empty, not good.

Sorrell made his way around too, moving fast.

I bumped up my pace and caught up with him halfway around. "How'd you go?"

"They all need filling." With his frown deep, he cast his gaze from the dry watering hole with its deep cracks to the barrels. "How do you fill the barrels when the hole is dry?"

"Hope holds the water skill and can lift large quantities of water in a floating bubble. She brings the water in from the river bordering our property, and Silas 'ports her about as she fills them." I crouched and checked the last barrel. Empty too. Rising, I ran my palms down my black leather-clad legs. "I'll ask her to drop by here as soon as she can."

"I can't see a great deal of cattle in this field." One hand raised to his brow, the sun harsh on the horizon, he scanned the plains. "Actually, I can't see any."

"Most of the stock graze along the fields closest to the river, but during roundup they follow the main trail right through this field. Do you recall the river where I first took you this morning? Because that's the river which runs right alongside our boundary and sustains life for this station."

"I remember." He tapped his head. "I stored the image so I can pop back there at any time. I have a few other images, from my visit last week, but I'm not sure those places are the same as where I might find you."

"Some of them will be, but I'll make sure you've got them all."

"Where's the kid?"

"He's exploring." I removed my Stetson and flapped my face. The breeze lifted sweaty strands of hair from my forehead and around my neck.

"It must be a huge job looking after this station."

"Yeah, but Hope and I wouldn't want to be anywhere else, and one day soon the rain will come and when it does, this land will flourish again."

"I can't imagine these dusty fields flourishing." He arched a brow. "You have a great deal of healthy optimism inside that pretty head of yours."

"You think my head is pretty?"

"Did I say pretty? I meant big." A cocky smile lifted his lips as he stepped closer. He settled a finger under my chin. "I've got the 'porting image for this spot now."

"Thanks for saying yes."

"To what?"

"To being my Destroyer. Finding the right one for me has been all-important." Unable to help myself, I leaned into his touch. "Thanks for not saying anything to your prince or my family either. That's huge too."

"Do you find it difficult to rest at night? With the dreams of foreboding, I mean?"

"I've recently installed floor senses in my room."

"Which means yes." He stroked his knuckle down my neck.

"It's becoming more difficult to differentiate between true wakefulness and if I'm still asleep. My dreams can be incredibly fragmented."

"Do the floor senses wake you up?" A stroke back up.

"As soon as I trigger them with my footstep, I get an electrical jolt. I haven't gotten past them yet."

"Which is good, but what happens if you 'port straight from your bed to the door. Do the floor senses reach that far?"

"No, they're only under the carpet around my bed, within three or four feet."

"So theoretically, you could jump over that in your sleep?"

"Yes, but why would I?"

"Chasers, in the past, have always changed their behavioral patterns to suit their needs." The breeze rose and he caught a lock of my flying hair and tucked it behind my ear. "I can hook up some door senses if you like, which would increase your coverage zone. I'll pick them up and install them for you tomorrow."

"You don't mind doing that?"

"You've got an entire station to run. I can handle the door senses. It's only one small chore."

"Okay, great." I set my hand on his arm, his bicep warm and large and full of hard muscle. "I like that I can talk to someone about this now. I've been keeping this secret for so long and it's been such a burden."

"You can talk to me about any—"

"Goldie!" Saunder tore from the trees in a jerky run, a brown snake flashing through the dry grass on his heels.

Aggressive and fast, it zigzagged with a hiss.

I sprinted, caught Saunder around the middle and gritted my teeth as the brown snake clamped down on my arm. Damn it.

Sorrell swung, his blade in hand.

Blood spurted, thankfully not mine. The snake though didn't survive my Destroyer's swipe.

I tossed Saunder atop my mount, made sure to get him out of the way, because where one snake roamed, more always lurked. Thankfully though, all remained clear, the copse quiet and no more snakes whizzing out.

"Let me take a look at your wound." Sorrell tossed both halves of the snake away.

"I'll be all right." The deep bite marks throbbed, but I'd get over it. My fast-healing skill would see to that, and hopefully soon.

"What kind of snake was that? It moved fast."

"It's an Australian brown snake. They're considered the second most venomous land snake on Earth. If it bit Saunder, we'd have to get him to a hospital fast. He'd need the anti-venom pronto, whereas all I need to do is wrap my arm with a pressure bandage. That'll slow down the spread of the venom until my fast-healing kicks in."

"There aren't any bandages, Goldie." Saunder had already

searched through the saddlebags from atop my stallion.

"It's okay. I can manage without them until we get h—" My vision wavered, the poison pulsing through me. I wobbled, swaying under the heat and the swiftly moving venom. I crouched next to one barrel then plopped onto my bottom and leaned my back against the drum.

"Are you sure you don't need the anti-venom?" Sorrell did a quick search of the saddlebags on the other horse, but came up empty handed. He hauled his shirt over his head and with his dagger, cut strips through it.

"I-I've been bitten a few times. No anti-venom n-needed."

"You're slurring your words." Fear widened Saunder's eyes. "Sorrell, you need to wrap her arm fast."

"Did you see any more snakes, or just the one?" I asked Saunder.

"There was one female snake near a clutch of eggs, so I thought I'd better see if there were any more. I didn't want any of our stock suffering a bite and dying. I searched deeper within the copse of trees and found five snakes altogether, four females and one male. I didn't mean to get chased by one of them, just figure out how many were in there."

"It's okay. I would have checked to see if there were any more snakes too. Don't forget that brown snakes aren't just aggressive, but territorial as well, and if they're short on rodents and rabbits nearby to hunt, then they'll track whatever they can." Whenever I could, I imparted lessons to Saunder.

"Got it." A firm nod from the lad.

"I'm glad we don't have snakes on our world. How many times have you been bitten?" Hunkered in front of me, Sorrell wrapped the strips he'd torn firmly around both sides of my wound then knotted it once done. He stuffed the remaining strip of his shirt's neckline in the back pocket of his worn leather pants and oh my—shirtless, with all his muscly-muscles on gorgeous display, my mouth watered.

"Goldie?" He waved a hand in front of my face. "I asked you a question."

"Huh, you did?" I shook my head. "Could you repeat it?"

"I asked, how many times have you been bitten?"

"Twice when I was younger, before I came into my fast-healing skill, and once since, now twice. These snakes are prevalent in the outback." I nodded at my makeshift bandage. "Nice work."

"I'd say anytime, but I'd rather not have to rip another shirt to bits for you."

"It was already ripped."

"But still wearable. That isn't the case anymore." He glanced at Saunder. "You all right?"

"Yep, but my dad got bitten by a brown snake last week near the river and he got really light-headed, his vision all skewered. It took him four hours to recover, and he's a fast-healer like Goldie."

"I see." He gave me a fierce frown, the lines across his forehead dragging down deep. "Why don't you eradicate these snakes?"

"They might have a deadly bite, but they're still creatures of this Earth and I would never attempt to eradicate them. I could have even gotten that one off me, which would have been far better than killing it. Next time don't jump into using your blade quite so fast." I pointed at the trees, which had doubled in number and now swayed all over the place, doing things trees just couldn't do. "Um, I'll return tomorrow and relocate the other four snakes to another location where the cattle won't come within striking distance of them."

"I'll be here to help you." His tone brooked no argument, so I gave him none.

My arm throbbed and I truly needed to get back on my horse, somehow.

I tried to get my feet under me, but got nowhere.

"Stay still. You're not moving in your current condition." Gripping my shoulders, Sorrell eyed me with a firm look.

"I'll stay still, but only if you take Saunder home first. I want him out of here where he can't get bitten."

"Sure, then I'll be right back for you. Give me one minute."

"Thanks." Getting bitten sucked.

"One minute," he reminded me with a jab of his finger. "That's all I'll be."

"I'll stay right here."

"Make sure you do." After a quick look at the trees, he bounded onto my stallion behind Saunder. A dig of his knees into the horse's flanks, and he galloped away before building up his speed. He shimmered and disappeared, 'porting fast.

Less than a minute later, he returned in a whirl of dust, just him, no horse. He collected his mount and brought it around in front of me.

"I dropped Saunder off at the corral. Guy asked if he was needed and I said I had you covered."

"Thanks. Saunder's such a good kid, and Guy is actually a bit of a worrywart. He's mated to Silvie, Silas's sister who has the fire skill. Do you know Silvie?" I was rambling, but it couldn't be helped.

"Everyone knows Silvie. She's the best cook. I love her fresh jelly donuts."

"I love them too. Silvie pops by here all the time." I shivered, even with the intense heat, my vision blurring further as the venom kicked in with more strength than I'd ever suffered from a bite before.

"Hey." Crouching in front of me, he flicked his fingers. "Goldie, stay with me. Keep talking so I know you're okay."

"Sorry, I'm still here, although really woozy."

"I'm going to carry you, all right?"

"Carry me where?" I pushed his hands away.

"To the horse."

"I can walk perfectly fine, thank you very much." That's if I could find my feet. They were supposed to be at the end of my legs, only everything twirled and I couldn't quite make them out.

"No, you can't."

"Yes, I—"

Muttering, he scooped me from the ground and hefted me into the horse's saddle. He settled in behind me, then with his arms looped around my waist and his reins in hand, he set off with a gallop. "Hold tight." He leaned in, bent his head close to my ear. "We're 'porting."

"Wait." My belly already churned at the ride alone, and would be far worse with a 'port. Barely holding the contents of my stomach down, I rested my head back against his shoulder.

"Do you feel sick?"

"Yes. Could you give me a few minutes before you 'port?" I rubbed my belly, which definitely helped.

"Sure. When everything settles, tell me." He breathed deep, his nose pressed to my neck.

"What are you doing?" I lifted one arm and sank my hand into his silky hair. And what was I doing?

"You smell nice, like sunshine and wind and something else." Another deep breath, his nose tickling my neck. "Vanilla. There's a trace of it on your skin."

"I like vanilla bubble bath in my bath." Which was far too much information and oh boy, I really liked the muscled warmth he emitted at my back. So wicked. His strength surrounded me and I relaxed further against him.

"Close your eyes if you need to." He tightened his hold around my middle. "I won't let you fall."

"I haven't fallen off a horse since I was five."

"You don't have to act tough around me." Curt words in my ear, although when I half-turned to eye him, a slight smile shimmered in his eyes even though his lips remained straight.

"I like the color of your eyes." I didn't mean to blurt the

words out, but the blue rimming the edge had melted further into the depths of the gray. Such an exquisite color. "They change depending on your mood."

"I have only one mood—emotionless. That snake bite has surely done a number on you."

"I like the color of your hair too. It shimmers with varying shades of gold and light brown."

"What the hell are you talking about?" His grumpy face made me giggle.

"Your locks are really soft and silky as well." I ran my fingers through his hair again, the horse flying across the plains where tumbleweeds blew across the land, the sun sending a final flare of red across the darkening sky. Night was falling.

"If you don't cease talking, I'm going to toss you from this horse." He gripped my hips as if about to do just that.

"Haha. You're so funny."

"You're clearly feeling better to give me this much sass. I'm 'porting us now. No being sick. I'm already out of a shirt and I don't want to be out of a pair of pants as well."

"Those pants could use tossing with all the nicks and slices you've got in them."

"The nicks and slices give me more movement." With no further warning, he made the swift jump and took us directly from Gullaroo to the field surrounding the stables, and thankfully my belly had settled enough for the 'port. No heaving for me. After trotting into the corral, he brought the horse to a halt, dismounted and tossed the reins to Guy. "I'll take Goldie straight to her room. Which one is it?"

"Upper floor. Right there." Guy pointed to my open balcony door, the white nets fluttering about in the breeze, then he squeezed my leg. "Hey, how are you feeling?"

"Dizzy still, but I'll be back to my usual self in no time at all."

"'Path me if you need anything."

"Some of Silvie's fresh jelly donuts would be great." I now had a craving for them since Sorrell had mentioned them. Yep, my belly had definitely settled.

"I'll ask her to rustle some up."

"I won't leave her until she's fully healed." Sorrell lifted me down from his saddle and keeping me bundled in his arms, made the swift 'port to my balcony. He stepped inside and juggling me against his chest, closed the glass slider.

"You can put me down."

"On your bed?" Striding across the snowy carpet, he eyed my bed made of redwood, the bedposts rising smooth and round to the ceiling with a white net canopy trickling over the edges, ready to be drawn down at night to keep any unwanted insects at bay.

"No, I'm dusty and dirty and will wreck the covers. I wouldn't mind a shower first since it's getting late. I'll lie down after I've cleaned up." I pointed to my attached bathroom. "That way."

"There isn't a chance you could stand up in a shower for long, if at all. Does Donaldo frequent this station?" he asked, his voice stern in my ear. "I don't wish to run into your father today."

"No, he leaves the running of this off-world venture to Hope and me. He always has."

"Good." He strode into the bathroom, gently sat me on the wide white tile edging surrounding the sunken spa bath and motioned to it. "A bath is a better alternative to a shower. There's no falling if you're already lying down."

"I'd love a bath." Perfect.

"I meant it when I told Guy I wouldn't leave you until you're fully healed. I'm supervising your bath." He plugged the hole and lifted the gold lever.

Water gushed out the spout, all steamy and deliciously hot. Exactly what I needed.

"Supervising duties don't include my bath time." I wagged a finger at him, a very wonky finger. "I'm not getting naked in front of you."

"Puh-lease." Grimacing, he shook his head. "You can bathe in your clothes. They need washing anyway."

"That's what a washing machine is for."

"Bathing with your clothes on is a great way to conserve water. I do it all the time in the mountains, and so do my men. We jump straight into the river with a bar of soap and get two jobs done at one time." He spied the bottle of bubble bath on the ledge over the bath and poured some into the running water. Gloriously scented vanilla bubbles foamed across the surface. "Do we have an agreement?"

"Conserving water is important." He had a point there.

Still grouchy-faced, he crossed his arms over his bare chest.

Oh boy, he could look terrifyingly good when he got feisty. I wet my lips since they'd dried completely out, then I ogled the rigid muscles of his pecs some more. "You've got a lot of muscles. I like that you do, unless I'm now hallucinating with this venom in me and your muscles are all just painted on."

"They're not painted." A smile cracked his face. "Your bath is ready, Princess."

"Put a shirt on and you can stay." I motioned to the door. "There are some spare clothes in the bedroom across the hallway, two doors down. Alexo, my brother, visits from time to time and you two are about the same ginormous size. Borrow whatever you'd like. He won't mind in the least."

"Stay right here. I'll be one minute." He walked out the door and my head got lighter then suddenly heavier, like a rock. I rested it back against the tile wall at my back, my eyelids sliding shut.

"I've borrowed one of his shirts and a pair of pants." He strode back into the room, dumped a blue tee and jeans on the corner wicker chair, turned off the lever and swirled a hand through the bubbly water. "This is the perfect temperature. Let's get in."

"Hold on. You said supervise, not that you'd bathe with me."

"I'm as dirty and sweaty as you are." He knelt at my feet, loosened the laces of one boot and popped it off before slipping the other free. Hands on my sword belt, he unstrapped it, set it aside and removed my daggers too.

"By the way, it's not polite to tell a girl she's dirty and sweaty." He needed to be put in his place.

He chuckled and I gave him my own grouchy-faced frown, which only made him laugh harder. With his own weapons set aside and boots kicked off, he aided me to my feet.

"We're getting far too cozy." I sagged against his chest, my legs barely supporting me, and his spicy, leathery aroma swirling all about.

"That bite has turned you weird. This isn't us being cozy. It's called getting the job done."

"I think my fast-healing is kicking in. I always get loose-tongued and say weird things when I'm healing and coming out the other side of an injury. I can get giggly too." I rubbed my nose against his pecs and breathed in more of his wicked scent. "You smell good for being so dirty. Do you say weird things when healing?"

"No, never." He swung me into his arms, stepped over the rim of the spa bath and settled me amongst the bubbles at one end, then slid down into the water at the other end. Our pant-covered legs rubbed against each other's.

"Could you shampoo my hair?" I couldn't stop my giggles from rising. My big, beefy Destroyer was lying in a bath of foamy bubbles with me. I couldn't have imagined this happening even if I'd tried.

"Shut up." Another fierce growl as he nabbed the shampoo bottle and squirted some on the top of my head. He dumped a handful of water overtop then scratched his fingers through my locks before dumping more water over me.

Soapy bubbles washed down my face and I spluttered through them. "Conditioner too. Please," I remembered to add.

"Gah, I hate you." A dollop of conditioner and he suddenly gentled his touch as he smoothed it through my hair, his knees bent and knocking into my knees.

I wriggled right around, doing a one-eighty so he could reach my hair better, then I leaned back against his chest as he drenched his own hair with water then scrubbed and rinsed. I got splashed with shampoo in one eye, but I didn't care. My muscles had relaxed and the throbbing in my arm had eased, the haziness in my head too. I pressed the spa button and soft jets of water pulsated into my sides and the soles of my feet. The jets would be massaging Sorrell's back, and going by his suddenly satisfied moan, I'd say they were definitely working a wonderful number on him.

My heart lifted, my mood even more so. I half turned around and looked into his eyes. "How do you like the outback so far?"

"I prefer the mountains where solitude reigns."

"There's plenty of solitude here. You can't deny that."

"There are a ton of snakes as well."

"Loads of poisonous spiders too."

"I hate spiders." He shuddered, one arm tightening around my waist, his other arm lying along the rim.

"Are you scared of them? Spiders that is? Lots of people are."

"I'm not scared of anything. I just hate them."

"Everyone is scared of something."

"Nope, not me." He cocked a challenging brow. "What are you scared of?"

"I've never taken the life of another before, but with my skill that's going to be inevitable one day. I'm scared of doing that, going too far and never being able to return from that dark place all Chasers go to. I love my family and I never want to leave them." Unfortunately, all Chasers succumbed to the kill sooner or later. There wasn't one Chaser who hadn't, not in all our world's history.

"I'll make sure to guard you well, so you'll have as much time as you can possibly get."

"Have you ever killed anyone before?" I slumped back against him.

"I've only maimed my enemy during battle, never killed." He scrubbed a hand along his bristly jaw. "Why do you ask?"

"Just wondering." With a long sigh, I lifted my gaze to the ceiling, my shirt and leather pants lying slickly against me. Such bliss. I stretched and soaked some more, the aches in my body slowly receding and my fingers tingling. I twiddled them to get more feeling back. Thank heavens for fast-healing, although even with that skill it wouldn't ease my tiredness. Only sleep did that at the end of each long workday. "I'm also scared of ants," I murmured into the silence. "I've never told anyone else that before, not even Hope."

"What the hell? Ants?" He chuckled, his chest bumping up and down behind my back. "They're some of the smallest creatures about."

"They're disgusting and far too resilient. They make me shudder when I see them."

"You're a wuss."

"Yeah, but think about it. Where there is one ant, there are actually a million more close by, a huge nest of them."

"You're still a wuss." He finger-combed my conditioned hair.

"Thanks." I splashed him and he caught my hand.

"Hey, you're using your bandaged arm. Is it finally healing?"

"Yep. It's feeling much better." I twisted fully around in the water and legs crossed, faced him, the jets which had been massaging my feet now swishing water into my back. With my arm extended, I tried to undo one of the many knots so I could remove the bandages.

"Here, let me help you." He tore at them, using his teeth on a couple of the more tighter knots, then he unwound the strips and dropped the soggy mess into the bath. He examined the length of my arm, although whatever swelling that had been there, had now definitely gone, the bite marks having healed and sealed over too.

"It looks good. Don't ya think?" I turned my arm from side to side.

"Yep, I agree." A decided nod. "My job here is done."

"Goldie?" A knock, and Hope peered around the open bathroom door, a plate of fresh jelly donuts in hand. Her eyes went wide as she spied Sorrell, a hundred questions clearly burning within her gaze as she turned it on me. "Guy 'pathed me and said you'd been bitten while checking the water barrels at Gullaroo, but not that you were taking a bath with your rescuer. He asked me to pick up some fresh jelly donuts from Silvie and drop them off to you." She slid the plate onto the wide tiled edging of the bath.

"Thank Silvie for me." I chose a donut with pink icing and lashings of cream then bit into it. Oh my, my taste-buds went to town. To Hope, I said, "I couldn't get my rescuer to leave, but I do highly recommend his maid services should you suffer a bite too."

"I am not your maid." He shoved water at me, which gushed over my face, although thankfully missed my donut since I jerked it away in time.

I wiped the water away, another giggle tearing from me. "Hey." I straightened my face as quick as I could. "Maids don't irritate their bosses."

"Again, I am not your maid." He pinched a donut with blue

icing, wolfed it down and followed it with a second.

"Okey-dokey." Hope smiled as she leaned one arm against the doorjamb. "What about the water barrels?"

"They need filling as soon as you can manage it."

"I've got an hour spare now. Silas and I will head out there pronto. Be good," she called out as she left. Her footsteps tapered away, my bedroom door clicking softly shut behind her.

I lolled back in the bath and polished off my donut. Done, I lifted and rested my feet in Sorrell's lap and with a gesture to my toes, smiled nicely at him. "Foot massage, please."

"One can tell you're a pampered princess." A grumble, but he still gripped one foot and kneaded into the soft flesh of my sole.

"I don't even know what 'pampered' means." I caught one of his feet and returned the massage. "I bet Hope has already telepathed Faith about catching us in here. They'll all think we're an item soon."

"We could work that to our advantage." He swished in and around my heel. "Then I could come and go as I pleased in order to check on you."

Hmm, that kinda worked for me too, particularly since more guarding meant his ability to keep me on the straight and narrow rose. I gave him a nod. "Okay, let's work that angle."

"Done, and we need to wrap this bath up." He rose, water sluicing down his bare chest and black pants. Out of the bath, he bounded and nabbed the plush white towel from the rail. He hooked it around his waist and with it secured in place, foraged in the vanity cupboard. Second towel procured, he tossed it to me, which I snagged out of the air. "Out you get. I need to make sure you can stand on your own with no issue before I leave."

"I'm fine, honestly." I stood and although a touch wobbly, found my feet and stepped out of the bath. I slung the towel around me, water pooling at my feet from my wet clothes.

"I'll decide if you're fine. Get dressed and I'll meet you in your room." He turned off the jets and pulled the plug.

"You are a very overprotective Destroyer." I bundled up my weapons and watched my step as I walked with care into my dressing room. I stripped out of my wet clothes, dried and changed into my favorite white nightshirt patterned with gold stars. It wouldn't hurt for me to hit the sack early, even though it had just gone dark.

When I came out, Sorrell stood in the middle of my bedroom in a pair of Alexo's jeans. He hauled a blue tee over his head, which fit him to perfection, all snug and outlining his hard muscles. With his hair combed back and the shaggy blond ends brushing his shoulders, he cast his assessing gaze over me.

"Do I pass muster?" I asked as I slipped between the sheets.

"You'll do." He flicked off the light and plunged the room into darkness. Or almost darkness. A trace of moonlight shimmered through the nets and sprinkled a pattern over the carpeted floor. He eased onto the other side of my bed and settled down, his head on my spare pillow.

"What are you doing?" I rolled onto my side and shoved one elbow into the mattress. "You're lying in my bed."

"Correct, and I'll hang around until you fall asleep."

"There's no need to."

"I'll also be back tomorrow to help you relocate those other four snakes."

"You don't have to."

"I want to."

"Are you a professional snake catcher now?" I leaned forward and almost bumped my nose into his nose. I was still a touch light-headed, but I'd be fine by the morning for sure.

"Nope." He clasped my shoulders and eased me back onto my back. "Although I wouldn't mind learning how the catching and relocation is done. It sounds interesting."

"I have snake forks and nets in one of the sheds. Catching and moving snakes is done on a regular basis around here,

particularly when the odd snake tends to sneak into the stables."
I yawned, turned on the switch above my head for the floor
senses, then snuggled my head into my pillow.

"You're clearly exhausted. Go to sleep. I'll leave once
you're napping."

"I've noticed that you like ordering me about a lot."

"You're the one who's been doing the ordering. Run the
bath water, Sorrell. Wash my hair. Massage my feet." A light
chuckle as he rolled onto his side and draped his arm around my
waist. "Now, go to sleep. I've only given you one order
compared to the ten you've given me today."

"You must be up to twenty, and I like giving orders." On a
dreamy sigh, I closed my eyes, my exhaustion quickly taking me
over. With no energy left, I slowly drifted, the lateness of the day
and the comfort of having him at my side, drawing me deeper
toward sleep.

Chapter 3

Chasers must choose their Destroyer.
Destroyers must make the blood oath of acceptance.
Death eventually comes for the Chaser.
That is the way of a Chaser's assassin skill.
No one can be judge, jury, and executioner.
Not even those who believe they are killing future murderers for
a just cause.
~ Recorded within the ancient tomes of Dralion.

So many images swirled through my head, sucking me into a dark void as I slept. I stood on my balcony in my white nightshirt, overlooking the eucalyptus trees swaying near the feed sheds, the midnight sky above a jewel of darkness overhead, the hot mugginess of the night surrounding me. Moonlight bathed the open range, while far in the distance a dingo howled, its call being answered by another dingo somewhere closer by.

"Goldie!" Saunder waved from the main door of the stables, a grin slashing his face. "The mare, Matilde, is in labor. Dad's overseeing the birth. You have to come now. Hurry, hurry."

"I'm on my—"

Saunder jerked forward and gripped his chest. Blood spurted from his mouth and his eyes rolled until only the whites showed.

I 'ported and caught him in my arms as he toppled forward.

A dagger protruded from his back and I could barely breathe.

I searched the darkened interior of the stables, caught the barest movement within, no more than a shadow within the shadows.

Gently, I laid Saunder down on the ground and fists clenched, stepped over his lifeless body.

Kill. I had to kill.

Who the hell had slaughtered one of my loved ones?

"Goldie?"

I shook with rage and—no, someone was shaking me.

"Wake up, right now." More shaking, my teeth rattling. "Come back, this instant. It's just a dream. Snap out of it."

I tried hard to break the spell of the dream.

I forced my eyelids open.

My vision cleared further and Sorrell wavered into view before me. Over his shoulder, the glass slider remained open and I stood on my balcony, not near the stables at all. "W-what happened?"

"You jumped right over the floor senses, then shoved the slider open." With his grip on my arms firm, he leaned in. "You've had a dream, a nasty one by the looks. Tell me what you saw, and be specific, because you look ready to kill."

"Someone killed Saunder." The words left my lips, no more than a dry rasp, my heart heaving. "One of the mares in the stables went into labor and Saunder—" Grief washed through me, hard and fierce, no matter it had all been just a dream. "The killer murdered an innocent lad. Saunder took a dagger to his back, a killing blow. Blood everywhere."

"Saunder is alive and well. There isn't a murderer here, and your dreams are merely dreams. They're interchangeable, provided we set a different set of events in motion. We have to catch the killer, before he kills. I promise you, no matter what happens, Saunder will never die." He wrapped his arms around me, stroked a soothing hand down my back, his warmth penetrating through and easing the chill in my blood. "Did you see anything to give away the date or time of this attack?"

"It happens the night Matilde goes into labor," I muttered into his blue shirtfront. "She's one of our mares. Saunder was beckoning me to come. He never misses a birth. It's like he has a sixth sense for when the mares go into labor. He said to hurry, that his father, Tawson, was overseeing the birth."

"That gives us a ton to work with."

"Saunder can't be allowed anywhere near the stables the night Matilde goes into labor." I'd never permit it.

"When do you expect that to happen? How far away is she from giving birth?"

"She's due this week, so any day within the next seven to come." I seized the loops of his jeans and held on with a fisted hold. "We've actually got three mares due this week, and Tawson has them all in one of the larger stalls. He's sleeping in there with them at the moment, while Saunder remains in the barracks with his uncles. Tawson is in charge of the breeding mares, and he takes his job very seriously."

"Then we'll leave Tawson with the mares in the stall at night, but we need to get Saunder out of here and back to Dralion. He can't be permitted to return until after Matilde gives birth to her foal. That's the part of your dream we can change."

"I'll ask one of his uncles to take him home for a short vacation with his extended relatives. How do we capture the killer? Whoever the murderer was, he or she kept to the shadows within the main holding room of the stables. I have no idea who it is."

"Then I'll camp out there each night until he or she shows up."

"This is the first dream I've had which has gotten so personal." I rubbed my nose into the deep V of his tee, my cheek brushing his chest, the skin to skin contact so soothing. "Sorrell, I'm not ready for this to get so personal so quick. I'm not ready for the chase to begin, or to want the death of another so badly. I thought I'd have more time."

"You will have more time, provided I keep you from the coming chase, which is why I'll be the only one permitted to camp out in the holding room. As long as you don't kill the killer, you're safe. You have to allow me to deal any justice out." He lowered his mouth to my ear, his voice a soft whisper. "That's why you came to me in the first place. I might be your Destroyer, but until you go Dark, I'm here to keep you safe."

"Okay." I hugged him hard, my insides all a twisted mess.

"Do you need to check on Saunder?"

"Yes." Without a doubt, I did.

"Take me with you." He didn't release me, his hold tight.

"Okay." I zipped us straight to the barracks and snuck a look in on Saunder curled up in his bunk across from his two uncles, the men both sleeping soundly after a hard day out on the range. Tomorrow, Saunder would be out of here too, to a far safer place. I'd ensure it.

Squeezing Sorrell's hand, I sent us winging away to the large stall holding the three mares due to give birth this week. In the dark, only a touch of moonlight shimmered through the venting window up high near the corridor ceiling. I lifted onto my toes, snagged the stall door and with my chin over the top, took in Tawson sprawled on a bedroll in the corner. All three mares rested, including Matilde, absolutely none of the horses in labor. Perfect.

"Let's take a look around the holding room and ensure all remains clear." Whispered words as Sorrell clasped the hilt of his side sword and on soundless feet, crept down the darkened passageway.

I followed him into the main holding room, the double doors leading outside closed for the night. I strode past one wall lined with saddles and tack and stroked one of the long reins, while Sorrell checked behind the hay bales stacked on the opposite wall, the bales a dozen high and a good twenty wide.

With a firm shake of his head, he returned to me. "There's definitely no one here."

"Yeah, I agree, and my dream doesn't center around tonight, but when Matilde is in labor." All remained quiet, and I could sense to the depth of my soul that Sorrell and I were the only ones here. I inched closer to him, rested my cheek on his broad chest and softly sighed as he wrapped his arms around me once more. "Sorry for being so clingy tonight."

"It's understandable."

"Who on earth would want to kill an innocent child? That I don't get."

"Possibly one of your enemies?"

His question grated on me. "I don't have any enemies, personally, but then again I'm Donaldo Wincrest's daughter, so of course his enemies have always been my enemies."

"Great." He let out a ragged sigh. "His enemies within Peacio number into the thousands."

"Yeah, the war might be over, but that unfortunately doesn't mean the hatred between my people and yours is suddenly gone. Even you didn't like me when you first met me."

"I still don't like you." A chuckle, his laugh lightening my mood.

"Liar." I pinched his backside and he squawked and chuckled some more, the sound so rich and warm and touching my heart. "Careful, Sorrell. You're showing emotions."

"Which isn't good." His chuckle died away and everything went dark as he 'ported us both in a quick jump back to my bedroom. He closed the balcony door then gestured for me to return to bed.

I slid back between the sheets and stared at the ceiling.

Sorrell lay beside me then hit the wall switch over the

headboard and activated the floor senses once more, not that they'd been all that helpful earlier tonight.

"Why are you still here?" I murmured into the dark.

"I fell asleep. I didn't mean to." Moonlight trickled over his face through the nets, his brow deeply furrowed. "Not that I can leave now, not after that bad dream you had. I'll remain until the morning."

"Thank you for staying." I wriggled closer to him. Deep in my heart, I didn't want him to be anywhere else right now, and no other thought could have shocked me more.

Chapter 4

A few hours later, I awoke to sunshine streaming in through my glass slider and the fierce heat of the outback already rising for the day. Sorrell had wrapped himself around me, one arm firm about my waist and one leg hooked heavily over my legs. I tried to squirm to gain some freedom, only he wouldn't budge, not one single inch.

"Stay still," he grumbled and tucked me in even closer. "I'm not ready to wake up yet."

"Well, I am." I tickled my fingers along his stubbly jaw and smiled at the prickly sensation under my fingertips. A new and unique sensation, one I liked. "You need to shave."

He pushed one eyelid open, his lips lifting into a stunning smile.

"Stop it. You're emitting emotion again, and possibly more than I can handle."

"More than I can handle too." His smile widened as he smoothed his hand over my rumbling belly. "Are you hungry?"

"Yeah, and you should be too. It is the morning and breakfast calls." Butterflies abounded in my middle as he splayed his hand even wider over my belly. I covered his hand with mine, my fingers slipping through the gaps between his fingers. Oh boy, I really wanted to twine our fingers fully together, to hold hands with him and argh—what was I thinking?

I yanked my hand back. "Ah, how about you let me go? I need to get up."

"Sure, if you insist." He groaned as he rolled away, then swung his legs over the side of the bed and jerked to a halt, his feet dangling an inch from the ground. "Sensors."

"Right." I flicked the switch to deactivate them. "Okay, now you're good to go."

"Thanks." He stuffed his feet into his boots, laced them and stood. With a swift hand, he strapped his weapons on then brushed past the redwood bedposts at the end of my bed, his gaze on me as his step slowed. He halted completely, a frown taking his face. "This is weird."

"What do you mean?" I crawled down the bed and pushed to my feet at the end, my toes sinking into my soft mattress.

"It feels strange walking away from you, like I'm not supposed to." He smoothed one hand around my waist, right to the small of my back and gently caressed the spot. His gaze softened, the steely-gray of his eyes lightening to a dove-like color, the pale blue rimming the edge blending in so beautifully. Unspeakably long lashes framed his stunning eyes. "Although the night has passed and so has the danger along with it. Nothing happens within the daylight hours of your dream, right?"

"No, the killer only strikes when it's dark."

"Good, because I need to return home and check in with my team. After that, I'll be back with the door senses. While I'm gone, you organize Saunder's trip home to Dralion."

"Will do, but you could stay for breakfast if you'd like to. There's no need to disappear quite so fast." I leaned my arms on his shoulders, the extra height of the bed bringing me eye to eye with him. "Our homestead chef is away for another week yet and Hope's meant to be cooking today since I cooked yesterday, but both of us are excellent at whipping up bacon and eggs, and I make awesome toast slathered in butter and honey too. After you've eaten, then you can go and check in with your team."

"Eating breakfast with you sounds too cozy, so I'm going to pass." He touched his forehead to my forehead, his next words a rough whisper. "Are you sure you're fully healed from the snake bite?"

"Of course, and I make awesome hot chocolate as well." I hadn't tempted him yet and I desperately wanted to.

"I love hot chocolate." He gripped my hips, swung me from the bed then settled my bare feet on top of his booted feet. Holding me close, his hands still on my hips, he dunked his nose into my hair. "Except you said you liked coffee. Black. With three teaspoons of sugar. Is that still not the case?"

"It is, but I like hot chocolate more, and you said you liked tea in a fine bone china cup, with a matching saucer."

"Don't forget the blood in it." He laughed, a big throaty sound that made me want to hear it again and again, only his laughter died away and his frown returned. "Honestly," he muttered, "I didn't want to admit my love of hot chocolate to you in the arena, not while I was trying to slam you into the ground."

"You and Lieska would get along well. She loves hot chocolate, and slamming people into the ground."

"Who's Lieska?" A quirk of his brow.

"A warrior who usually works here at the station, although she's currently away visiting her family in Dralion. You'll get to meet her later next week when she returns."

"Actually, I believe I have met her. Does she have dark hair? And is she mated to one of my fellow protectors, Cole Cyrano?"

"That's Lieska."

"Then we've definitely met." A grunt as he set me aside then shaking his head, he walked into my bathroom.

"How'd you meet Lieska?" I followed and leaned against the bathroom doorjamb as he collected his soggy clothing from the floor where he'd left it after our bath.

Wringing the water from his bundle over the tub, he glanced over his shoulder at me. "Lieska holds the hunter skill, the same as Cole. They recently tracked down a lost Peacian kid in the woods near my mountains. They saved him before he perished. She's one of the good warriors from your country. She certainly gained my respect with her determination to find the kid."

"She can hunt down anything and anyone, and I only hang out with the good warriors."

He snapped his teeth together as he stepped up to me, his clothes shoved under one arm. "Protectors and warriors have been working together since the war between our countries ended, and it's strange to see."

"Strange, but good." Even I had to admit that.

"True, not that it's an easy transition to work with one's enemy." He growled again under his breath.

"Ex-enemy, and you seem riled."

"I have to leave and for some reason that's rubbing me the wrong way." He eased back a step, clenched his fists and bit out, "Don't go getting into any trouble while I'm gone."

"I'll do my best."

One narrowed look as he shimmered and disappeared.

My heart pinched tight at his leaving, my next breath coming harder.

Hmm, that shouldn't have happened. At all. Not one bit.

Rubbing my chest, I breathed slowly in and out until the discomfort eased.

It took a minute, perhaps two, but once I came right, I crossed to my slider and pushed the white lace nets aside. I opened the glass door and welcomed the new day that had dawned.

The gum trees beyond the stables swayed gently in the breeze, the trees more brown than green and needing a good dunking of water. I'd mention it to Hope and have her bring some here.

Far into the distance, the dusty red plains ruled the land, the golden heat of the sun shining bright over every inch of the station.

Yep, we had another endlessly hot outback day ahead of us.

I opened my link to Hope, as I usually did each morning once I'd awakened. *"Hey, where are you?"*

"Downstairs cooking breakfast. It's my turn and I want an update on Sorrell too. Immediately."

"He stayed the night." I returned to my bathroom, foraged for my brush and ran it through my messy hair, all knotted from the night before.

"How come?"

"To make sure I was okay after the snake bite." I secured my long golden locks into a ponytail with a violet hairband that matched the color of my eyes. A pinch of my cheeks to add a bit of color. Very helpful. I applied my favorite lip gloss, a cherry-red that tasted of cherries too. Sweet.

"Sooo, you really, really like him, huh?"

Since Sorrell and I had decided to utilize the liking pretense, which was becoming more truthful with each hour that passed, I said, *"Yep, but this thing between us is new. We're just feeling our way around things. He is a protector after all, so I'm not sure if anything long term could ever work out between us."*

We'd never have anything long term, not with my stupid, sucky assassin ability. Why had I even gotten dumped with it? No other Wincrest had held the skill before me. I certainly would have heard about it from my father otherwise.

Closing my link with Hope, I hiked into my dressing room. I changed into a pair of skinny cherry-red jeans to match my lippy then donned a sleeveless tan outback shirt. I added a red and tan checked neck-cloth I could lift over my nose in case the wind tore through and the dust swarmed, then I lugged on my boots and strapped on my sword belt.

Wrist daggers sheathed, I slapped on my black Stetson, opened my door and bounded downstairs.

At the base of the stairwell, I crossed the wide-open front foyer on the first floor, my boots tapping across the diagonal floor tiles of midnight blue. Recessed lighting lit the rich burgundy painted walls holding breathtaking landscapes of Dralion. I stopped before my favorite painting and smiled.

The black granite cliffs of home, with Wincrest Palace rising high behind those cliffs, a midnight sky reigning overhead, the moon far larger and more orange than Earth's moon. The palace stood four majestic floors in height, all built in gray-black stone and from each of the many corners, slender towers rose to double the height of the palace, fourteen towers in all. My father's residence was a fortress, impressive and stunning, the painter having captured it beautifully, with light even shining from behind the stained-glass windows along the lower floor. Such detail.

The granite cliffs, an impenetrable force and a natural wonder, ran alongside the ocean and stood unbroken for ninety miles either side of the palace. It would be wonderful to show Sorrell those cliffs, and the many places within Dralion I adored.

Hmm, not happening though.

He might be my guardian and Destroyer, but taking him places within my homeland would be more akin to actually dating him than keeping things professional.

Sharing a bed wasn't exactly professional either, although there had been a very good reason for doing so. He'd been worried about the snake bite, then accidentally fallen asleep. I'd had the awful dream of foreboding, so it had been extremely handy having him around to run a check of the stables with me. Yeah, a solid reason.

I left the painting behind and strode into the kitchen.

Hope sung a soft tune as she dropped bread into the toaster and poured two glasses of orange juice. She handed one to me as

I sidled up beside her, her look expectant. No surprises there.

"Good morning." I sipped, trying not to notice that expectant look.

"I want answers about you and Sorrell."

"Did you fill the barrels at Gullaroo?"

"Sure did." She tapped one foot, that expectant look doubling.

"You really need to dump some water on the gum trees outside too. They're about to keel over." Barely hiding my grin, I wandered through the swing doors leading into the attached dining room, the doors swaying shut behind me. Hope had already laid out plates and cutlery on the large oak dining table, as well as set a platter of bacon strips and scrambled eggs in the center. She had everything covered today.

I slid into the ruby padded chair at the end, hooked my Stetson on the back of my chair and served myself a portion of what Hope had cooked. I added some to her plate too, right as she swished through the doors with a plate of buttered toast.

In jeans and a blue and white striped shirt, she took her seat, a no-holds-barred look blazing in her violet eyes. "So, Sorrell Sona stayed the night. I want all the details. Right now. I'm not taking no for an answer."

She clearly wasn't going to give up on this conversation. I cut into my bacon, chewed then forked a mouthful of eggs. "Mmm, this breakfast tastes wonderful. You've done an excellent job."

"Have you two kissed?" She didn't miss a beat as she tore into her bacon strip. "You have to answer my questions, otherwise I'm going to go crazy with the need to know."

"No, of course we haven't kissed." I stuffed toast into my mouth and kept it full.

"But you two have bathed together, so something big is going on."

"We bathed while clothed," I muttered around my

mouthful.

"While barely clothed."

"We were definitely clothed."

"He's got a lot of muscles." She arched one teasing brow.

"You keep your eyes off his muscles and on your own mate's muscles, and speaking of your mate, where is Silas?" Silas usually ate breakfast with us before tending to his own duties for the day, whether they were here at the station, since he liked to aid Hope, or with Davio as he assisted his cousin with his royal duties.

"He's with Davio this morning. They're dealing with some secret wedding details, which Faith and I aren't allowed to know about. He'll be here in another hour or two."

The air swirled and the golden-edged ruby drapes either side of the wide bay window swayed. Faith and Silvie 'ported in, a monster three-tiered wedding cake between them.

"Make way, make way," Faith ordered as she sidestepped so she and Silvie could settle the cake on the table. "We've brought a surprise," she added with a flourish of one hand toward the cake. "This is the mini version of our actual wedding cake, a trial one to make sure we like all the layers Silvie has made. It's taste-testing time."

"We're eating breakfast." I stuffed a bacon strip in my mouth and mumbled around it, "We need to finish this first. Give us one minute."

"I'll grab the plates and cake forks." Faith disappeared into the kitchen, her golden locks pinned back at each side, her cropped yellow tee baring an inch of the slight rise of her belly, her white jeans sitting low on her hips.

I wolfed my breakfast down, just as Hope gobbled hers too.

"I've 'pathed Belle and she'll be here soon." Silvie swept around the table, her red-gold hair bouncing as she hugged Hope then squeezed me.

"Thanks so much for the donuts."

"You're welcome. I'd not long made a batch, so they were ready and waiting to be eaten." In her short red summer skirt and matching tank top, she perched on a chair, her elbows on the table and her chin propped in her raised hands. "Sooo," she drawled, her gaze on me. "I heard all about you and Sorrell, that he stayed the night. You two even had a bath together."

"I caught the same update too," Faith said as she returned with the dishes and cake forks in hand. She plopped into the chair between Silvie and Hope, her expectant look identical to what Hope's had been earlier.

"Can there be no secrets around here?" I glared at Hope.

"Hey." She held up her hands. "I didn't tell either of them."

"Then who did?"

"Silas told me. My brother has a big mouth in case you didn't know that." Silvie waggled her brow at me. "There are also no secrets permitted between us girls either, so you need to spill the details."

"Yeah, no secrets," Faith added as she hauled the cake closer then swiped a finger through the top layer of creamy icing adorned with violet iced flowers and iced gold ribbons. A long lick of her finger and she slapped her lips together. "Mmm-mmm, this is sooo delicious."

"Faith, you're supposed to cut into the cake with a knife, not consume it with your fingers. Sheesh, where are your manners?" Silvie picked up a beautiful ceremonial knife from the platter next to the cake and held it hilt-first toward Faith. An array of diamonds, rubies, and sapphires embedded in the fine steel, sparkled. "You need to cut into it with this knife too. It's special, and has been used to cut each and every Loveria wedding cake for over a thousand years."

"Wow." Wide eyed, Faith accepted the blade and turned it over in her hands as she studied it. "Although shouldn't I wait to use this blade for when Davio and I cut the actual wedding cake on our wedding day?"

"Nope." Silvie tapped the blade. "The bride always uses this ceremonial knife to cut the trial cake as well, and it's meant to bring good luck in the lead up to her wedding day, which is why I asked Davio's mother for it from the Jewel and Artifacts Vault. I polished and shined it up this morning. Now it's simply waiting to be used at your hand."

"Wait, there's a vault where the Loveria jewels and artifacts are kept?" Faith appeared taken aback, her chin dipping down and eyes narrowing. "How did I not hear about this?"

"You'll get access to the vaulted room once you're an official Loveria, and no longer a Wincrest. You're also trying to sidetrack this conversation."

"Ha, I'll always be a Wincrest, whether I'm married to Davio or not." Faith rested a hand on Hope's shoulder as she eyed her sister. "Since you and Belle have been going through Peacio's tomes lately, do you know anything about this knife? I've never seen one so beautiful."

"I can tell you anything and everything you want to know about it, although this is the first time I've actually seen it with my own eyes, other than for in a drawing." Hope accepted the knife from Faith and gently, carefully, turned it over in her hands. "There are records in Dralion about it too. This knife was gifted to the Loveria royal family before our Wincrest family went to war with them."

"Oh look, there's an inscription." Faith leaned in and traced some wording embedded along the length of the blade, barely discernable wording, but still there all the same.

"What does it say?" I asked her, my curiosity beyond piqued.

"Pirate Princess," Faith read out loud, then eyed Hope. "What does that mean?"

"This inscription was engraved into this knife by the giver of it, King Octavius Sol the First, the ruler of the Eastern Isles of our world."

"I've never heard of the Eastern Isles. Where are they?" Confusion marred Faith's brow.

"They used to lie to the east of Peacio and Dralion, although some say they never existed, but Octavius Sol the First certainly did. He first ruled the Sol desert tribe of No-Man's Land."

No-Man's Land being the barren expanse of desert land between Dralion and Peacio, the thin band of shifting sands governed by the Sol tribe, their land having divided our two warring nations of Dralion and Peacio since the very beginning.

"It's said," Hope continued, "that when Octavius Sol left No-Man's Land in search of more hospitable land, he discovered the chain of isles to the east and named them the Eastern Isles. He then became the ruler of them."

To share what I'd learnt over the years, I leaned forward. "I've read about the so-called Eastern Isles having existed, but there's absolutely no proof of it, even a thousand years on. It's like a magical place that might have existed, but if it did, then it simply disappeared."

"Wow, so there could be a magical place currently hidden from our eyes?" Excitement ringed Faith's voice.

"Yes, exactly." Equal excitement rung within Hope's voice as she answered Faith. "There's also a foretelling recited over this knife by Octavius Sol and it states that one day, far in the future, when the lines of Loveria, Wincrest, and Sol once more join together, that the Pirate Princess will sail the seas and arrive on our shores. That is when the Eastern Isles will be unveiled, and all shall see it once more."

"Incredible." A low whistle from Silvie as she gazed with intrigue at Hope. "In the tomes, is there any mention of what the Eastern Isles look like?"

"It's said the isles are scattered about the east and are a land of milk and honey, with people who hold skills we've never seen before. Or at least that's what's been recorded. Certainly, the tale about this knife has always fascinated me."

"It now fascinates me too." Faith held out her hand for the knife and after Hope handed it back, she inspected it with awe shimmering across her face. "There is so much I have yet to learn about our world of Magio. I want to meet the Pirate Princess."

"Maybe one day we will, that's if the foretold tale comes true." Hope motioned to the cake. "My mouth is watering and I'm about to drool all over this table. Cut it already."

"Okay, okay. I'm onto it." Faith sliced the knife through the top layer and removed a piece of rich chocolate cake. She plated slices for all of us, including one for Belle, our empath who'd yet to arrive.

"Don't eat too fast, or you'll get a belly ache," I warned as I slid the cake under my nose. Silvie's cooking was to die for, and the warning was as much for me as anyone else. Cake fork in hand, I dived in, exactly as the other girls did too.

"A-maz-ing. Thank you so much for this cake, Silvie. I love your cooking." Hope beamed at Silvie then knocked her shoulder into Faith's. "I need a slice from the middle and bottom layers too. We should sample all of the three cake layers."

"The middle layer is lemon buttercream, and the bottom is red velvet." Faith set slices of both the other layers on our plates, then dug into her own pieces. "Mmm," she moaned. "I think my favorite is the chocolate. What's yours?" she asked Hope.

"Red velvet for me. It's deliciously excellent, but the chocolate is a close second," she mumbled around a mouthful of all three layers. "I love how the lemon buttercream actually adds a tart hit that clears the palette for more of the chocolate and red velvet. Do you know what I mean?"

"Yep, I totally do," Faith garbled around her forkful. "The babies are asking for more of all three layers too. I need to accommodate them."

I laughed and ate.

"How come I can smell cake?" Guy strode in, red dust smeared across the front of his blue outback shirt. He made a beeline straight for Silvie as she ate and tipped her back in her chair before licking the crumbs from her bottom lip. "Mmm, is that chocolate cake, lemon buttercream cake, and red velvet cake I can taste?"

"Yes, and stop stealing it from me. Cut your own slices."

"I like stealing directly from you." Guy tipped Silvie back even farther and she squealed as she grasped his shirtfront.

"We're here for cake too." Belle breezed through the door, Nicolas at her side. She sat and grinned as Faith and Hope stuffed their faces. "It appears the cake is a hit."

"Help yourself." I pointed at the quickly disappearing layers. Belle was a protector and an empath who'd recently accepted the bond with Nicolas, one of my fellow warriors, an amazing healer, the two of them both a part of our world's new leading eight. Silvie and Guy, Hope and Silas, and Faith and Davio, made up the other six members, an equal number of warriors and protectors, all eight of them now entrusted with ensuring a smooth transition in the dealings between our countries now the war had come to an end.

"Nicolas, why are you glowing?" Hope nudged cake forks across to him and Belle. "Have you just healed someone?"

"He healed me, not that I needed healing." Belle tapped Nicolas's nose.

"You definitely needed healing." Nicolas fed Belle some cake then kissed away a smear of creamy icing from the corner of her lips. "Are you feeling better?"

"I bruised my knee, a tiny bruise that didn't require any healing."

"I can't allow my mate to suffer even a single bruise. That goes against who I am."

"Aww, stop being cute, and impossible to argue with." Grinning, Belle fed Nicolas a forkful of cake this time then glanced at me. "And what's this I hear about you and Sorrell being a thing?"

"Did Silas tell you?"

"Yep. I would never have picked you two as a mated pair."

"We're not mated." Silas needed his neck wringing. "We're just seeing each other."

"Oh, sorry, I must have understood. My mistake."

"*I'm back.*" Sorrell's deep voice bounced around inside my head. "*Where are you?*"

"*Downstairs in the dining room.*" My heart skipped a beat, which it really shouldn't have done. "*Listen for all the noise and chatter and you'll find me.*"

"*I've got the door senses, but I'll need an electrical kit to fit them.*"

"*I have one in the storage room below-stairs. I'll grab it for you later. For now, come and join us.*"

"*Who's with you?*" His tone rung with frustration, a touch of anger too.

"*Faith and Silvie brought a trial wedding cake with them. Belle and Nicolas have arrived, and Guy is here too. Is everything okay?*"

"*No. I've left the door senses in your room along with the clothes I borrowed last night. I'm coming down.*" Booted footsteps thumped down the stairs then Sorrell marched into the room. He'd changed and now wore a tan leather jacket, no sleeves, with two thick silver snake bands coiled around his biceps. His blue jeans sat low across his waist, the bottoms skimming a pair of tan ankle-high boots with chunky silver buckles. He halted at the end of the table and surveyed the crowd.

"*Nice armbands, and be prepared for an inquisition.*" I gestured for him to take one of the free seats. "Don't be a stranger."

"I don't eat cake." He remained right where he was, arms

crossed and feet planted wide.

"Is your team organized for the day?"

"I wouldn't have returned otherwise."

Oh boy, he was definitely frustrated and angry, although I had no idea what I'd done.

"Hmm," Belle murmured as she cast her gaze between the two of us. "As an empath, I can definitely feel the sparks flying between you two. Are you sure you're not a mated pair?"

"You're simply picking up on the fact that Sorrell hates that he likes me." I winked at my Destroyer. "Isn't that right, big fella?"

"You wanna fight?" Snarling, Sorrell slid his sword free and pointed it directly at me. "I haven't had the chance to fit in a training session this morning, and I'd rather enjoy going another round or two with you."

"Oooh, you're such a flirt." I stuck my Stetson on my head, pushed my chair back and slid my own sword free. "Meet me next to the corral." I'd battle his bad mood right out of him, or at least I'd certainly try to.

I flashed away and reemerged outside.

Sorrell zipped in and everyone else appeared in a shimmer one by one.

My chest tightened and I blew out a hostile breath, right in Sorrell's face. "Don't go easy on me. I'm completely healed from the snake bite."

"I hadn't intended on going easy. I need to vent some of my anger, and preferably on you."

"Yep, there are definite sparks. Belle's onto something there." Faith, her cake plate in hand, clambered up the railing to get a better view and perched on the top beam. She waved for me to continue. "Don't mind the rest of us. We all like watching a good training session."

"I don't." Hope gave me a fierce look, then Sorrell one. "Keep the training clean."

"I won't spill her blood, if that's what you mean by clean." My Destroyer strode back and forth in front of me, his sword fisted tight in his hand. "I'll give you ten seconds to limber up."

"That's so generous of you." A snarky answer, but I couldn't help it.

Nicolas climbed up next to Faith, then extended a hand to Belle and aided her up the railing.

Silvie and Guy took a position together under the swaying boughs of the nearest gum tree, Guy sneaking in for another kiss with her.

Bending and stretching, I swung my sword in a wide figure eight and loosened my muscles.

Sorrell sniffed the air, his nostrils flaring. "Your ten seconds are up."

"Come and get me then." I crooked one finger.

He canted his head to the side, like a predator sizing up his prey. "I might not eat cake, but I do eat my adversaries when they rile me."

"Okay, what exactly have I done to rile you since you left?" Because I had no idea.

"You've been breathing."

"Oooh, more flirting." Blade firm in hand, I moved in a slow circle around him, although he remained right where he was, his gaze on me as if he waited for me to attack first. "Are you being a gentleman and allowing the lady to go first?"

"Do it. Attack now." He gritted his teeth, his jaw clenched. "Or I'll be the first to pounce."

"I might like it when you pounce." I couldn't keep the teasing tone from my words. "Get ready to train with a real warrior, Sorrell Sona."

"Do you know of one?" He lunged and I heaved back, but not fast enough.

His blade sliced across my arm and blood spurted.

I whipped off my neck-cloth, wound it around the wound

and tucked in one corner to keep it secured in place. I'd suffered far worse hits on the training field and this would heal fast enough on its own, although Nicolas eyed me questioningly, the warrior healer in him likely needing to heal one of his own, particularly his princess. "No, I'm fine." I gave him a shake of my head. "I don't want to halt this fight." Which had barely begun.

"I shouldn't have done that. I apologize." Shock and fear cut across Sorrell's face. "I didn't mean to hurt you, Goldie."

"It's only a nick. Don't worry about it." I stepped farther back to give myself a few more precious seconds to heal before I recommenced our training session, although the sensation of my skin pulling together already tingled under the makeshift bandage.

"Goldie?" He seemed to hesitate. "If you want to stop, simply say so."

"Honestly, I'm fine." Where was my Destroyer? Clearly, I needed to rile him again. I swung and he met my attack, our two blades crashing dead center, then I dropped low and kicked one leg out. I hit him hard in the shin before springing back to my feet.

Huffing, he twirled and I struck again, my second hit far harder than the first. He even had to shove one foot back to brace himself against my strike, and giving him no further leeway, I came at him again, harder and harder.

I attacked, over and over without holding back.

Yes, it was time for my Destroyer to show me his true grit.

Chapter 5

"Cease trying to antagonize him, Goldie." Twenty minutes of intense fighting later, Hope barely sat still on the corral railing. "You're goading and taunting Sorrell."

"She's doing it for a reason." Sorrell pushed me back, and with my attention on Hope for a millisecond, cornered me against the railing and sheathed his blade. He tore mine from my hand and slid it into my scabbard, then pinning my hands to the highest rail above my head, the rest of my body held in place with his body alone, he muttered mind to mind, *"Aren't we supposed to be acting at least a little smitten with each other?"*

"Yeah, but I want to fight right now, not act smitten. And you started this battling session between us by turning up here all angry." I heaved against his chest, somehow managed to slip free of him and ducked under his arm. "Catch me if you can."

I raced away and he tackled me.

He rolled me across the dusty ground, one hand firm around the back of my head, the other my waist as he kept me securely tucked against him.

We tumbled to a stop, him on top and drat it all. I was completely trapped underneath him, his touch searing me deep inside. Never had I both raged for a fight, or had my heart beat so fast. "Something's wrong," I whispered. "With me."

"Something's wrong with me as well." He lowered his head

to mine and brushed his cheek against my cheek. "So many emotions are storming through me and I'm not sure how to process them all."

"Let me up." I wriggled as I tried to free myself.

"No, if I release you then you'll only wish to fight with me again." A fierce growl as he tipped his head to the side and cast his gaze on our current audience.

Hope appeared worried. Faith looked much the same. Silvie and Guy were smooching behind the tree, no longer interested in us but making out themselves, while Nicolas and Belle snuggled with a strangely knowing look. Although what that knowing look was about, I couldn't tell. This wasn't the place or time to quiz them either.

"We're out of here." I gave Sorrell no further warning, but 'ported us straight into the storage room in the cellar of the homestead. From blinding sunshine to a blackout of darkness, we arrived in the blink of an eye.

"Where are we?" he muttered, his cheek still pressed to mine.

"In the storage room below the homestead. The electrical kit is in here, the one you asked for so you can install my door sensors." I tugged and finally freed my hands. "You're very heavy. Move it, big fella."

"If I let you up, promise me they'll be no more fighting between us."

"I promise. No more fighting." He moved in the dark, only an inch, but the second he did panic roared through me. I wrapped my arms around his neck and clung to him. "Wait a second. I've changed my mind. You're not heavy at all."

"Do you feel it too?" His lips grazed my ear as he sank to one side, rolled us both over until I came up on top of him, our movement causing the motion sensors to flick the overhead lights on. He gazed up at the bright bulbs, then took a quick look around at the shelving units where they stood all the way to the ceiling with boxes stacked on them.

I tightened my hold around his neck and looked into his eyes. "Why do I feel suddenly lost when we're not touching?" It was the glaring truth, and I couldn't help but speak of it.

"When I nicked your arm before, I almost lost it." He gripped the neck-cloth I'd wrapped around my arm and tugged it down to my wrist, then gently he inspected the thin pink line where my skin had already sealed over. "August twenty-ninth," he bit out as he returned his gaze to mine. "That's the day, a little over a year ago, when I first felt driven toward this station. I got close enough to this homestead to overhear two of your warriors speaking of this land belonging to the Wincrests. After I did, I got out of here real fast. I've been ignoring the truth, and the pull of it every day since."

"The truth about what? And what pull?"

"Of the mated bond. One grows between us."

"No!" Everything swayed even though I remained still. There couldn't be a bond. "You're my Destroyer, and that's all. We can't be mated."

"When you got bitten by that snake, it almost tore my heart in two and this thing between us, Goldie, it's definitely the mated bond building. Even I can't deny it any longer."

"Are you sure?" Yet I couldn't miss the truth in his words, or the piercing pain in his voice at making the admission. Or the fact he'd sensed that bond over a year ago and done nothing about it.

Argh, how frustrating.

I heaved off him, shoved to my feet and blew out a long breath. I glared furiously at him for good measure too. "I don't want to be soul-bound to you. I'm a Chaser, with a death sentence hovering over my head."

"I'm well aware."

"You're my Destroyer. I expect you to destroy me one day."

"Again, I'm well aware." He glared right back at me.

"You can't destroy me if we're mated. It's impossible for those who are soul-bound to hurt one another."

"I'm as upset about this as you are." He threw his hands in the air and paced from wall to wall.

"You need to leave, and never come back."

"I can't."

"Of course, you can." I jabbed a finger at the door. "Head right out that door. You put one foot in front of the other, and don't look back. That's how you leave."

"I can't leave while you're this upset."

"Sorrell, you never intended on seeking me out. I came to you when I needed a Destroyer. I don't want a mate and can never accept one." A stabbing spike of pain settled around my heart. Dismissing our bond wasn't going to be easy, not now we'd spent time together, except we clearly had no choice. He had to go.

"I agree. I was born to be your guardian and Destroyer, not your mate, but you do need me. I can sense it to the depths of my heart and soul." He caught my arms, stroked gently up and down.

"We're incredibly mismatched. What we need to do is release each other from this bond."

"You still need a Destroyer." His gaze intensified.

"You have a brother. I'll ask Asar to take over the position. It was always going to be one of you. I'll simply accept my second option." My pulse rocketed. His warm hands on my arms and the intense look in his eyes was all for me, and I liked it, even though he was all fired up and frustrated.

"I know my brother well, and Asar would agree to the request." He touched his forehead to my forehead, his voice scraping on the last word, as if he fought his emotions.

"You are so incredibly annoying."

"Yes, I can be, and you'll need to be firmer with me if I'm

to leave." He lifted his head, his gaze resolute on mine. "Goldwyn Wincrest, I hereby release you from our mated bond. No longer do I wish to be yours, or for you to be mine. You may choose whoever you wish to bind yourself to in the future, no matter how long that future will be. I certainly wish you only the best."

I didn't hesitate with my response. "Sorrell Sona, I hereby release you from our mated bond. No longer do I wish to be yours, or for you to be mine. You may choose whoever you wish to bind yourself to in the future, and I too certainly wish you only the best."

"Good. That'll help." He stepped back, his hands fisted at his sides. "We need time apart, except I have the door senses to install and I never break my word once given. I also promised to aid you in the capture and relocation of the snakes. Then there's staying in the stables at night, until the mare goes into labor." He cast his gaze to the shelves. "Which box is the electrical kit in? I'll get that job done first."

"There's no need for you to fit the senses." Hot tears burned at the back of my eyes, but I shoved them back. "Or carry out any of the rest of your promises to me. Hope and Silas can help me with the snakes, and I'm going to send Saunder back to Dralion with one of his uncles, as we agreed. Tawson is already sleeping in the stables, and I'll ask Asar to take the holding room in your place."

An easy answer, and I waited for him to give me his agreement. Certainly, speaking our release of each other was just the beginning. Remaining apart over the coming days and weeks ahead was essential in breaking those first anchors we'd already placed in each other. Only time apart would truly aid us in widening the gap and moving on from each other.

He continued to look uneasy, his fists opening and closing, his jaw clenched and a muscle in his jaw ticking away. "We did the right thing, Sorrell. You need to leave."

"Yes, we did do the right thing in releasing each other."

"You'd already decided to let our bond pass, particularly since over a year ago you ignored your need to find out exactly who you were mated to." A tear leaked past my guard and I ducked my head before he saw it, then I nabbed the box with the electrical kit and lobbed it to him. "Fit the senses, then go. You're relieved of any other duties."

I had to send him packing, and I needed to do that now.

Chapter 6

"You down there, Goldie?" Hope bellowed, her footsteps following with a firm *thump* as she strode down the cellar stairs.

"Yeah, I'm here." I opened the storage room door, Sorrell right behind me holding the electrical kit.

She marched inside, her Stetson in hand and her gaze lobbing from me to Sorrell then back to me. "I need to know exactly what's going on between you and Sorrell. That wasn't a normal training session, not in any way, shape, or form. You too looked extremely close for a moment, which actually made me happy, then you flashed away and now I'm worried, truly worried."

"Nothing is going on between us." I gave Sorrell an insistent look that said *hurry up and agree.*

"She's right. Nothing is going on." Scowling, Sorrell stormed out the door, his booted footsteps pounding up the stairs.

I went to follow, only Hope blocked my path and wouldn't move. "Where's he off to in such a hurry?"

"To fit some door senses in my room."

"That doesn't explain the tension between you two." She crossed her arms and gave me her interfering look. "Why would you even need door senses?"

"Because we're mated and he's worried about my safety."

"Huh?" Her blond eyebrows launched into her hairline.

"Did you say mated?"

"Yes, in the way of a mated pair, which we weren't expecting, and aren't actually keen on. We're not a good match so we've released each other." I dived around her and raced upstairs. "End of discussion," I yelled back.

"Hey, you can't just blurt that out and run off." She chased after me, her Stetson stuffed back on her head and her blond hair flying from underneath it.

"That's exactly what I'm doing." I made it upstairs then walked face-first into Silas, who had cake in his mouth and a plate piled with even more cake on it. "Why are you everywhere, Carver?"

"I heard yelling and came to investigate. My mate sounded mad."

"Hope is mad." I tried to push past him, but he remained adamantly in place. "You protectors are annoying, always getting in my way."

"Goldie and Sorrell are mated," Hope announced with a wheeze as she rushed in. She stood next to Silas then turned on me once more. "You've finally found your chosen one, and now you've decided you're not a good match. That doesn't make sense. You had a bath with him and he stayed the night. You fought out in the training yard with grim determination, and if you ask me you're incredibly well matched. You both like fighting and hacking into each other."

"They're mated, huh?" A conceding nod from Silas as he cast his gaze at me. "That kinda makes sense considering Sorrell wished to see the place last week, and now this week the two of you are hanging out. What's not a good match about you both?"

"Everything!" I also had no intention of getting into specifics, not when I'd have to explain I was a Chaser with an assassin ability and a short lifespan. Not happening. Not ever.

"Goldie, you need to listen to me." Hope shook her head, her cheeks all flushed and eyes blazing. She was clearly not happy. "There's a reason our souls are bound to each other's. You two simply need some more time to talk. Don't go ending things just yet." She tipped her gaze to Silas and with a frown, wiped the crumbs from his chin. "That's good advice, right?"

"It's the best advice, and I'll speak to Sorrell and ensure I make that clear to him as well, that they both need to give each other more time." Silas popped a kiss on Hope's nose. "I'll find him and speak to him."

"He's in Goldie's bedroom, so you don't have to go too far."

"Really?" A snicker from Silas as he glanced at me. "Are you two sure you've ended things?"

"He's installing some door senses, a safety precaution only, then he's out of here." I caught Hope's hand and glared at Silas some more. "I'm taking Hope with me to Gullaroo field. There's a nest of snakes slithering around the trees near the watering hole and we're going to relocate them to Wandaroo Rocks, where the cattle don't roam."

"Sounds good. I'll catch up to you two there once I've spoken to Sorrell." He bounded up the stairs.

I marched outside with Hope and followed the path to the horse corral. Kicking at the red dust underfoot, I muttered, "Some people simply shouldn't be together and Sorrell and I are two of those people."

"I'm finally getting to know Sorrell, and there's so much more to him than what I first thought. Following your snake bite, he looked after you, and when the two of you were battling in the yard together, it was impossible to miss the shock and pain that crossed his face when he slit your arm. You've always wanted a mate too, and don't tell me you haven't."

Grrr. Not only had we grown up together, but Hope knew me better than anyone else and yes, I'd always wanted a mate, but not after learning about my assassin skill. I unclipped the gate and waited as she came through, then clipped it again.

She tipped her Stetson back and eyed me, one hand still on the brim. "When I first met Silas, I never thought a bond between us stood a chance, not with the war that raged between our countries. I released him, which was the worst mistake I've ever made, and I'm glad we retracted that release and committed ourselves to our bond. Give Sorrell a chance. It won't hurt to take some more time before making an absolute decision."

"August twenty-ninth." Cupping my hips, I sent a breath whistling out. "He wrote that date on the back of the photo he took of the watering hole, and it's the date from over a year ago when he first sensed a mated bond forming with someone here at our station. He never intending on seeking me out back then, not when he ran, and he wouldn't have sought me out now if not for the fact that I turned up in his arena and challenged him to a fight. His first instinct was to drop me, which means he doesn't get a second chance."

I couldn't ask him to remain either, not when I intended to ask his brother to take his place as my Destroyer. When I eventually went Dark, I'd be pitting two brothers against each other, and that I could never do. Sorrell would want to keep me alive, and Asar, as my Destroyer, would be fighting Sorrell to end my life, as Asar would eventually have every right to do.

"It doesn't matter how you first met, only that you did."

"Wrong, and I totally disagree." A light breeze swirled, the gum tree's leaves fluttering overhead as the sun blazed down. All remained quiet near the horse corral, none of the others in sight as I turned on my heel and marched down along the path. "Where'd everyone go?" I asked Hope as she jogged in beside me.

"Nicolas and Belle are still officially on their honeymoon, taking time off whenever they can. Nicolas mentioned something about taking Belle to a secluded island in the middle of the South Pacific for the rest of the day. I'm picking Fiji, but he wouldn't disclose the actual location. Faith and Silvie took the remainder of the cake home before Silas ate it all, and Guy's running a check on the cattle down by the river." She nabbed my hand and hauled me to a stop. "Sorrell isn't going anywhere until I say he can."

"You're not allowed to get stroppy with me."

"You're like a sister to me, and I love you. I don't want to see you getting hurt and giving up on your bond will be more than hurtful. It'll be a pain that could rip your heart and soul in two." She thumped her chest, her hand fisted and knuckles going white. "I know. I've been there and done that. Give your mated bond some more time before you toss it away."

"Sorrell doesn't want the mated bond with me. He spoke the words of release first, so I chased it up with my own."

"Yet where is he right now?" She pointed to my open balcony door on the top floor of the homestead higher on the hill.

Sorrell had stepped outside with a screwdriver in hand, wires now running down the slider. Silas leaned his jean-clad butt against the balcony rail, his back to us as he said something to Sorrell I couldn't quite pick up.

"Seeing to your protection," she continued with a mutter.

"Look, I understand where you're going with this conversation." Although no matter what she said, nothing would change the decision we'd made.

"If he didn't really want the bond, he'd have cut all ties immediately and taken off. He's got to be hurting too, incredibly confused as well. It's difficult when the bond strikes and our feelings get all mixed up."

With his teeth gritted, Sorrell cast me a frustrated look over his shoulder before getting back to his job at hand. I heaved a long sigh. "I'll talk to him later, let him know your thoughts."

"You'll do more than that." Hope rimmed her hands around her mouth and yelled, "Sorrell, dinner is at seven tonight, in the dining room. Our homestead chef is away on holiday and Silas and I are cooking. There'll be you, Goldie, Silas, and me. No exceptions. You got that?"

"I'm busy," he growled back, then jammed the screwdriver into the slot.

"Then un-busy yourself, mister." An annoyed huff from Hope. She caught my hand and dragged me toward the sheds where Saunder's pet, a stray sheep dog that had appeared on our doorstep six months ago, snoozed in the shade with his dark head resting on his brown and white paws.

Saunder. I had to get him away from the station, as soon as I possibly could. I'd sort that out now. I scooped up the dog's empty water bowl and refilled it from the outside tap before setting it back and patting the dust from his coat. I gave him a good rub down as I opened a link with Tawson. *"Hey, I need a favor."*

"Name it and it's yours."

"I'm organizing something special for Saunder, but he can't be here while I'm doing that organizing. It's a party for his fourteenth." With Saunder's fourteenth birthday only a week away, that sounded completely plausible, and we'd definitely be having a huge party once I'd sorted out all my problems and dealt with the killer coming my way. *"Could you ask one of your brothers to take Saunder home to Dralion and to stay there with him until I say Saunder can return?"*

"Of course. I'll get onto that right now. He'll love having a party."

"Excellent." I closed our link. Phew, that was one all-important job out of the way.

"Who are you talking to?" Hope stood over me, arms crossed and one foot tapping away.

"Tawson. I asked him to ask one of his brothers to take Saunder home to Dralion for a bit. I want to organize a surprise birthday party for him, and he can't be here while I'm doing that." I pushed to my feet and shoved open the creaky wooden door to the shed. Once inside, I swiped a crate, set it underneath one of the high shelves housing the gear I needed and bounded onto it. I collected a snake fork and canvas bag, jumped down and gripping Hope's hand, zapped us straight to Gullaroo and the copse of trees housing the inhospitable snakes. We'd catch the critters we didn't want this close to the watering hole and water barrels, and ensure our stock remained safe. "You ready to catch some brown snakes?"

"Yep, but they're the worst to catch. They move so fast and they're so aggressive." Hope held out her hand for the bag and I passed it to her. We'd always worked together incredibly well, like a well-oiled team when in snake catching mode.

"We've four more snakes to catch. Saunder noted five yesterday and one is already dead. Sorrell's fault. He sliced its head off when it attacked me." Within the cluster of gum trees, dry, stalky grass waved at knee height in some places, while in others it remained flattened out.

"I bet Sorrell didn't know that we prefer to catch and release any snakes we find." Hope rubbed my arm. "He would've been acting on his mated instincts, his need to protect and such."

"He mentioned when I got bitten it almost tore his heart in two."

"See, and I'm not surprised. Silas would've been the same, lopping that snake's head off." A knowing nod.

"Let's go in slow." Lowering to a crouch at the edge of the tree line, I tipped one ear inward, my battle skill gifting me with advanced hearing. A swirl of wind and a hiss reached me on the breeze. "Okay, I've got one snake at twelve o'clock."

"I wish I had advanced hearing like you do. It must be awesome." Hope readied the bag, opening the top, her gaze focused at the twelve o'clock mark.

I tapped the fork lightly on the ground, enough for the snake to pick up on it and wonder if a small creature had entered its hunting ground. A brown snake slithered through the grass and we both jumped into action.

As it lifted up to attack, I jabbed the two prongs either side of its head and shoved downward. It hissed as I caught it, the underneath of its head flat to the dry grass and my fork caging it completely in place, the rest of its body slithering about in protest.

Hope scooped the tail up with the bag then slid the canvas under its belly and ballooned the bag over the snake's head. "You do the count down," she advised.

"Gotcha." I gave her a nod and murmured, "On the count of three. Three, two, one, go."

I released the snake and Hope whipped the head fully into the bag and twisted the canvas top to keep the critter trapped inside. She grinned wide. "One down, three more to go."

"I'll 'port this one away and release it." I took the bag from her then made the quick jump through time and space to Wandaroo Rocks, a rocky hillside at the very outskirts of our station where the cattle never roamed. I left the bag on the flat between two large boulders and bounded onto another boulder close by, the fork in hand and prongs extended in case the snake turned on me and made another strike.

With the bag opening free, the snake slowly slithered out, gave a last hiss in my direction then slunk behind the scattering of rocks beyond the bag.

Once assured it was gone, I collected the bag and zapped back to Hope.

I shimmered in next to the trees where I'd left her and argh, Silas and Sorrell were here, Silas holding a second fork and bag, Hope right beside him. As soon as Silas spotted me, he tugged Hope into the trees and disappeared.

How annoying.

"They're ganging up on us." With my fork and bag in hand, I trudged across to Sorrell with a long sigh. "How'd the installation of the senses go?"

"Very well, and yeah, they're both clearly upset we've released each other." He snuck the bag from my hands, a consigned look on his face. "I'll be here for dinner."

"I'm sorry they're being so stubborn about our decision to release each other."

"Silas was peeved, and I got the entire story about how he released Hope when they first met and that doing so had been the greatest mistake of his life. He warned me not to make the same mistake too, that we need to give our bond some time." He hunkered down and snapped off a dried yellow flower from within the stalky grass then rose and tucked it behind my ear. "Now, they can't say I'm not trying."

"You're so romantic." I dug the fork into the ground and smiling, snagged the flower and plucked one crusty petal from it. I sent it twirling away on the breeze. "He loves me." Another petal, my smile widening. "He loves me not."

A chuckle and Sorrell tweaked my nose. "They don't understand our circumstances, that's all."

"He loves me." Another petal to the wind. "Nor will they ever understand us either, not when I can never come clean about…well, you know about what." I dropped the remains of the flower, jabbed my heel into it and crushed it into the dusty dirt and grass. "He loves me not."

Giving him my most determined look, I gripped the fork and marched deeper into the trees. "It's time to catch us some snakes. There are still three left to find."

"Sure, let's do that." Amusement flickered in his eyes. "Have I ever mentioned I find a tough and dangerous woman, sexy?"

"You dated Belle before she accepted the bond with Nicolas. She's an empath and anything but tough and dangerous."

"She appears that way, but in fact underneath her gentle heart is a woman who's as tough as nails. She stood up to

Donaldo Wincrest during the final battle between our kings, so she's definitely tough. I'm also certain she could have tamed my hardened heart with no issue at all, that's if she'd given Nicolas the flick like she'd intended on doing and agreed to date only me."

"It's a real shame you let her get away." I liked Belle, and had from the day we'd met. "Did you ever kiss her?"

"No, and Nicolas couldn't stay away from her when he should have, but you won't find me making that same mistake with you." His voice had lowered to a rough whisper. "I'm still here for one reason alone, and that's to keep the promises I've made. After I've fulfilled those promises—helping you here with the snakes, dinner, and sleeping in the stables until Asar has things covered—then I'm outta here."

"You don't have to fulfil any of those promises."

"I do."

"You don't." A snake hissed and a slither of silvery-yellow streaked through the grass. The snake lifted its head, fang teeth dripping and forked tongue flicking out. I thrust and wedged the prongs into the hard ground either side of its head. "Don't move too fast, Sorrell." I kept one eye on the snake and the other on him as he swept around beside me.

"Tell me what to do."

"You need to scoop the snake's tail into the bag first, slither the canvas under its belly then pull the bag over its head. You won't be able to bag the snake all the way because of my prongs in the ground, but you'll get most of the creature in."

"That snake isn't brown." He came in behind it, dipped the tail into the bag then followed through with the belly before scooping the canvas over its head, just like he'd done it a million times. More hissing, both from the snake and Sorrell.

"Australian brown snakes can vary in color, from fawn to black, including the colors of orange, silver, yellow, and gray. Most brown snakes though are a uniform shade of brown, but they can still have various patterns, speckles and bands."

"Calling them brown snakes is deceiving."

"Yeah, you're right." I couldn't keep my smile at bay. "This is fun, huh?"

"Hey, we've got one bagged!" Hope yelled from somewhere farther within the trees, somewhere slightly out of my sight.

"We've got another one too, almost," I called back.

"We're 'porting to Wandaroo Rocks to release our one." Hope appeared along the track from between the trees, her jeans all dirty and a streak of red dust smeared across her forehead and the front of her blue and white striped shirt.

"What did you do? Dive on the snake?"

"Yep." She grinned as Silas emerged with the bag and fork.

"We'll be back in five minutes." Silas nodded at me as he caught Hope's hand. "Stay safe."

"You too." They both shimmered away, and I pinned one of my hands over Sorrell's holding the bag in place, my heart skipping a beat at the renewed touch of his skin against mine. As I looked into his eyes, it skipped a second beat. So aggravating. I cleared my throat and muttered, "Let me take over with that bag. I don't want you getting bitten."

"I can handle a snake bite." His grim look said he wasn't relenting. "Tell me what to do next."

"You are a stubborn protector."

"Yeah, I am, so get used to it."

"I actually like that you're stubborn." I conceded that information with a long sigh. "Which is truly annoying."

"It's tough being mated." His voice softened, his grim look too. "Although I can handle all of this if you can."

"We'll tough it out for the rest of the day, but tomorrow is a different story. If I catch you on this land in the morning, I'm gonna slice your head off. No questions asked. Straight off." I sliced a hand across my throat. "Do we understand each other?"

"Yes, and you're talking sexy with all this head slicing. It calls to the Destroyer in me." He sliced a hand across his own throat, a grin lifting his lips. "Cease and desist all of that talk."

"You cease and desist."

He chuckled and motioned to the snake. "Tell me what to do next."

"First, I going to remove the fork and when I do, the snake will attempt to strike out. You have to be quick in bundling its head into the bag, then you twist the top of the canvas so it can't escape. It can't sink its teeth through the canvas itself, not when this bag is designed for this very purpose. Are you sure you want to give this a go without seeing how it's done first?"

"I'm a quick learner." He gave me a nod. "On the count of three."

"Wait." Even with the snake hissing away, I couldn't help but smile during the intense moment, my heartbeat racing in anticipation of the snake's capture. "Do you mean counting down from three, like three, two, one, go? That's how I count down."

"I don't have a 'go.' I move on the 'one.'" He snapped another dried flower from the grass and tucked it behind my ear. "She loves to torment me."

"Stop giving me dead flowers." I grinned, my words coming out with a giggle.

"You want a live one?"

"Do you even know where to find one?" The thought of him picking me a live, sweet-smelling flower, doubled my grin.

"My mother's garden. She's got green thumbs and is always tending to her beloved flowerbeds. In my youth, I hauled more plants around than you could ever imagine."

"What's your favorite flower?" What a fascinating insight into his childhood, and I eagerly wanted to hear more, no matter the riled snake.

"The bloodroot."

"I've never heard of it."

"The plant has a bright white flower."

"A lot of plants do. What makes the bloodroot plant special?"

"The flower actually gets its name from the bright red poisonous sap that flows from the stalk once it's cut."

"Oh, now I see why it's your favorite." A deadly plant. So obvious.

"Yeah, it's a killer." He eyed the snake, his look going serious. "We better finish off catching this thing, or are we going to chat all day?"

"I would love a flower garden." Haha. His serious look turned peeved in one second flat. He was so easy to rile. "Except that's impossible out here in the outback," I continued as if we had all the time in the world to chat. "The sun fries every living thing that bursts from the ground as soon as it sprouts."

"If I have to kiss you to shut you up, I will." A threat, one issued with a challenging lift of his eyebrow.

"You wouldn't dare."

"Wanna bet?" He leaned in, until our noses touched. "One more outspoken word from you and I'm all action."

Not a chance did I want that action.

I pinched my lips shut tight, then whispered mind to mind, *"Three, two, one."* I tugged the prongs free on the "one" just as he'd asked, not the "go" which I left off, and he whipped the snake's head into the bag and twisted the top like a pro. I bounced to my feet. "Yay! Great job. Hand me the bag and I'll transport it to Wandaroo Rocks."

"No, you can 'port us both there. I wouldn't mind knowing where the release point is for the rest of the snakes."

"There's only one more snake to find, and are you always this argumentative?"

"Pretty much." He gripped my hand. "Zippedy-zap now."

"Hey, we're back." Hope ducked along the dry, grassy path

and joined us, Silas one step behind her as he kept a lookout within the undergrowth. Interest gleamed in her violet eyes as she spied our hands linked. "I see you've got your snake. That leaves one more to find, right?"

"Yep, and we're going to release this one now." I tried to shake my hand free of Sorrell's, only he tightened his hold on me. Goodness. When he set his mind to something, he never backed down.

He shook his head, his next words whispering through my mind. *"You got bitten yesterday by one of these snakes. I'm coming with you. 'Port us now, and that's an order."*

"You have to learn to be more accommodating." Although I gave in and flashed us both to the rocky hillside of Wandaroo Rocks. We arrived under the searing heat of the afternoon sun, only the odd tuft of grass protruding from around the plethora of boulders and rocks, the hillside falling away into a deep ravine with a shallow creek at the base. Deep cracks in the creek's basin sucked at the remaining water within, while on the other side of the creek the dusty plains ran for miles upon miles. I motioned to those plains, tumbleweeds blowing across the land and heat swirling from the ground like a vapor. "That spread belongs to our neighbors, although this hillside is ours."

"How many cattle do you rear here?"

"Due to the drought, we've had to reduce our stock, but when it rains again we'll be able to bump our numbers back up to thirty-five thousand head. We're currently a little short of that." I removed my Stetson and the breeze lifted my ponytail from my neck and blew it about. Oooh, so nice. Shielding my eyes with my hand against the bright ball of the raging sun, I moaned. Not so nice. "One either loves this land, or hates it."

"I can see the beauty within it, no matter the drought." He held up the bag in his hand, the snake having gone quiet within. "How do we release this critter?"

"It's all about gentle placement and running. They might be

snakes with a vicious bite, but they're still creatures we need to look after, and they're incredibly helpful in keeping the rodent and rabbit numbers down. Find a flat spot, lay the bag opening away from you, then release it and get well back, preferably somewhere behind me. I've got the fork, so I can jab it again should it attack."

"Right. Will do." He picked his way around the stones to the flat spot where I'd released the last snake then he hunkered down with the bag and winked at me over his shoulder. "This spot look good, Princess?"

"It sure does." I bounded onto the closest boulder.

"Let's get this girl out of there then."

"It's not a girl. It's a boy."

"How can you tell?" He released the twisted opening and jumped onto my boulder with me, right behind me as instructed with one hand around my waist as he kept his gaze locked on the bag.

"I paid attention when we caught it. Look at his tail when he comes out." The silvery-yellow snake slithered free of the opening and slipped across the stony ground then disappeared around another boulder several feet away, his tail flicking and hiss gentle.

"What am I looking for?"

"You can tell he's a male by the shape and length of his tail. The male's tail is thicker and longer than the female's, and it tapers differently. It's thick, then suddenly thins out to the tip. The female has a thinner and shorter tail than what the male has, and it tapers evenly to the tip."

"Interesting. Got any other valuable information I need to know?"

"Yep, male snakes engage in what's called 'ritual combat' with their other male counterparts for control of certain territories, that being the territory they consider their particular backyard. The most dominant male will chase off all the other males in the area then mate with the remaining females." I reached up on my toes and ran my fingers along his firm jaw, the stubble tickling my fingertips. "We're in the peak of mating season right now, and the first snake that bit me was a female, the others we've captured all females too. The last should be female as well, which means he will have been the only male in that copse of trees. Now, we need to find four nests belonging to the four females and relocate their eggs as well."

"I hope we're talking one egg per snake?" His questioning look made me laugh.

"Snakes are very productive while in season."

"Two eggs?" A hopeful arch of his brow.

"A female snake will produce a clutch of ten to forty eggs, although she has nothing to do with her young once they hatch. The juvenile snakes raise themselves, living or dying under their own steam."

The wind stirred and Hope and Silas shimmered in a little farther along the rise. Silas held his canvas bag high, his red shirtsleeves rolled to his elbows. With his Stetson shading his face, he called out, "We got the last snake, a female. Now we're after four nests."

"I just explained that to Sorrell." I waved out.

"Which we'll find," Hope added as she gestured for Silas to set the bag down farther away, which he did then hopped back onto the same boulder Hope had jumped onto. The female snake slithered away with a flick of its tail and after she did, Silas collected both his sack and ours before extending his hand for my fork.

I passed it across to him with a, "Thank you."

"No problem." He caught one hand around Hope's waist, his gaze on me, "We'll 'port back to the station and collect a couple of crates to transport the eggs from the copse to this rocky hillside. Hopefully, we'll be able to find the nests quickly and with no issue."

"I hope so too." The two of them shimmered and disappeared. I faced Sorrell. "Once this job is done, I need to speak to Asar. I want him here tonight, so you don't have to be."

"I'll 'path him, let him know you want a meet-and-greet, although no matter if he's here or not, I'm staying as promised for tonight. He can cover the rest of the nights until Matilde goes into labor on his own. Although there really needs to be a smooth transition as I hand over my duties to him." He grazed a finger under my chin. "Letting go of you won't be easy, but I know it needs to be done. I won't be around tomorrow. Will that work for you?"

"Deal. That way I won't have to slice your head off."

"Ha, as if I'd let you get in a killing strike. Let me try and reach Asar now and update him." He tapped his head and closed his eyes, and I waited as he spoke to his brother.

The wind played with his hair, brushing it back and forth over his shoulders and I itched to slide my fingers through it as I had before.

Eyes open again, he nodded. "Asar's on duty until ten. I gave him the run down, and he's on board. He's certainly shocked about our bond forming, but definitely on board."

"Excellent." I gave in and lifted up onto my toes, slid my fingers into his hair and buried my face in his neck. "Thank you for reaching out to him."

"Anytime." He growled rough and low, his own arms banding fiercely tight around my waist. "Everything will be all right." A gentle stroke down my back. "We can handle this release and parting of ways."

"Yeah, and ignore my clinginess. It'll pass."

"Only if you ignore my need to let you cling." He nipped my ear and I almost sighed with delight.

I certainly smiled as I pulled back an inch. "Do you want to 'port us back?"

"Yep, to Gullaroo we go." He zipped us through the dark

and released me as soon as we bumped down in the blazing sunshine.

"This way." I gave him my back and strode into the trees in search of the nests. The first was an easy find since it lay within a hollow of dried grass, right under a gum tree. On my knees, I carefully leaned into the hollow and passed one egg back at a time to Sorrell, who cocooned them to one side on the grass.

"We're back!" An echoing shout from Hope.

"We're here," I answered then waved as she ducked around a bush and appeared.

"Found you." With a wide grin, Hope set a crate next to Sorrell and helped him carefully transfer the eggs inside, while Silas added some to the crate he carried.

Several feet away next to a dip in the ground where the earth was loose, Silas spied another nest and got down on one knee.

"Lookie, we're on a roll." Hope hurried across to Silas and helped him scoop eggs and set them inside their crate.

I wandered around and found the third nest, then got to work passing the eggs out. Sorrell stacked them inside the crate with the others and I couldn't miss his lightened mood, not a frown in place and only a smile lifting his lips. I tapped his arm with the back of my fingers. "You're enjoying yourself, aren't you?"

"I've never done this before and honestly, it feels good giving these creatures their freedom and a new future elsewhere, these unborn ones as well."

"Are you sorry you killed that first snake?"

"No, not when it bit you." He thumped his chest with one balled fist. "In that moment, it made itself an instant enemy to me."

"I get that now." I stood and wiped my hands on my jeans, the cherry-red holding patches of grimy-brown on the knees from all my crawling about in the dirt, grass, and leaves. "I need another bath," I muttered as I walked onward in search of the last nest.

I shoved bracken aside and peered into bushes, while Silas and Hope shuffled about within the undergrowth close by, Hope's occasional squeal sending the birds in their nests above soaring high.

"You two need to stop having so much fun," I grumbled and grumped at them. "It's very distracting."

"Sorry." Hope poked her head out of a bush and smiled at me, not looking sorry at all. "This last nest is proving difficult to find."

"You keep searching on this side of the copse of trees and we'll take the other side." Onward, I continued, Sorrell carrying the crate behind me as he searched too.

Finally, we found the last nest after scouring every last inch, the nest well hidden within an abandoned rabbit hole, of all things. I shoved my arm down the hole and fumbled around within the depths of the hollowed basin, then carefully plucked out eight eggs from within reaching distance, only there had to be more, for sure. We'd been averaging twenty eggs per nest.

"Let me have a go." Sorrell plucked me from the ground where I'd been lying down on my belly and set me back on my feet. With a smile, he rubbed the tip of my nose, his thumb coming away with a streak of dirt.

"How are you not sweating and getting all hot and flustered?" I snorted under my breath. He appeared gloriously cool, calm and collected with his tan leather vest no longer laced, but open and exposing his bare chest, not a drop of sweat on him, while I was drenched under my arms and down my back.

"That's because you've been the one doing all the huffing and puffing this afternoon. I'm just enjoying the view of your backside up in the air while your head is down each hole."

"Enjoying the view of my backside isn't going to help you long term." I poked him in the chest. "We're not together, remember?"

"For some reason, it sure feels like we're together. You're grumbling at me, exactly as my mother grumbles with my father, and I'm feeling pretty special because of it." A wink as he got down on one knee and slid his sword free. He stabbed the dirt around the opening of the rabbit hole as the afternoon sun blazed. The ground crumbled and he swept it away before it caved inward, then he continued making the hole bigger.

Hope breezed in with Silas lugging their crate and perked up at the sight of our find. "You uncovered the last nest. I didn't think we were ever going to find it."

"Neither did I." I motioned to their crate. "You can take that to the base of Wandaroo and find a natural hollow in the ground which will do as a new nest. Make sure the eggs remain out of harm's way."

"Will do. We'll head back to the station afterward, grab a late lunch then head to the river. I'll dump some water on the gum trees around the homestead and the watering holes in desperate need of it." She hugged me then eyed Sorrell. "Don't forget. Seven sharp for dinner. You're expected."

"I won't forget." He saluted her. "I give you my word I'll be there."

"Perfect." Grinning, Hope joined Silas and together the two of them shimmered away.

"I'm starving. What about you?" I checked my watch. It was almost three, the lunch hour well and truly past.

"My belly's been rumbling for the past hour."

"Mine too." I knelt next to Sorrell at the enlarged entrance he'd made to the rabbit hole. "Do you think you can reach all the way in now?"

"I'll give it a go." He got down onto his front, the silver snake bands curling around his biceps pinching into his muscles as he flexed them with his longer reach.

I played one finger over the silver band gracing his left arm.

It held an inscription which read, *Our greatest battles are those with ourselves*. Very true. That could often be the case. I leaned over his broad back and caught the inscription on the other band, this one different to the first. *Only you can control your own happiness*. Double true.

"Where'd you get these bands? I love the inscriptions on them."

"They've been handed down from the eldest son in the Sona family to the next eldest son, for several generations."

"They're a family heirloom?"

"Yep, and there's a second set of armbands which my mother gave to me at the same time my father gave me these. They're for...ah…never mind."

"Are the other armbands inscribed?"

"They're identical to mine, with the same inscription, only slightly smaller for a woman's arm." He grunted and shook his head. "Nope, this hole is clear, with only eight eggs. My fingers are sweeping the entire cavity."

"Okay, then we can call this job done." I rocked back onto my rear, sat and wiped the back of my hand across my brow.

He righted himself, sat on his backside too, and rested his arms on his raised knees, his gaze on me as he took a moment to catch his breath. "I'm gonna take a swim in the river behind my cabin after we've taken care of these eggs. Do you want to join me? I can make sandwiches."

"No. Yes. No." I crawled closer and swept a finger over his dirty chest. "You shouldn't have made that offer. We've released each other. There's only one dinner meal to get through to make Hope happy."

"One meal and one night. Don't forget my promise to stay in the stables. I haven't broken a promise yet, and I don't intend on starting now." He stood then with the crate in hand, pushed one elbow out. "Take ahold and we'll 'port together."

I did, curling my fingers around his bent arm, right before

he sent us winging away through the dark to the base of the rocky hillside.

Carefully, he picked his way around the rocks and halted as he spied a hollow protected from the elements between two boulders. A tip of his head toward it. "Does that spot look good to you?"

"It's perfect." I crouched next to him and together we gently settled the eggs inside the large hollow and stood back with wide smiles after the job was done. I brushed my dusty hands against my cherry-red jeans. "Thanks for all your help."

"It feels good to have done this." He swung the empty crate from one hand, his gaze moving over my head to the plains in the distance.

"Here, let me take that so you can wing your way back home. You said your belly was rumbling." I snuck the crate from his hand and held it snugly to my chest. "I, ah, hope you enjoy your sandwiches and swim."

"Are you sure you don't want to join me?" He pinched the crate back and kept it out of my reach behind his back as he swayed from foot to foot. "My entire team are on duty and we'd have the river all to ourselves. The water's so cool and refreshing, crystal clear and deep as well. I also make awesome roast beef sandwiches."

"Stop it, that sounds far too tempting." Not only would I adore a swim, but I could eat a horse right now and the sound of those sandwiches had my mouth watering. I reached around him to nab the crate, but he kept it out of my reach.

"Do you have a swimsuit in your bedroom, Princess?"

"Yes, but—"

He snagged me around the waist and everything went dark. Moments later, we arrived with a swirl of wind in my bedroom, the sun's afternoon sunshine shimmering through the nets over the balcony slider.

He set the crate against the wall and strode straight into my dressing room. "Where is it?" he called over his shoulder. "The swimsuit?"

I marched after him. "In the top drawer of my dresser, but honestly—"

"Got it." He pulled a one-piece white swimsuit from the drawer and tossed it to me, then flipped through the racks of my clothing and selected a long, lacy white summer dress with crisscross straps at the back, as well as a pair of leather flats from the shoe rack. With my dress folded over his arm, he stepped up to me. "I've even got you a change of clothes for after your swim."

"What if I want to wear jeans?"

"Then I'll switch this dress to some jeans." He snagged a pair of jeans from the rack, a shirt too. "That better?"

"No, I'd rather wear the dress."

"You're arguing with me just for arguments' sake." He rehung the jeans and shirt.

"Yes, I am." I had no problem admitting that either.

"You can use my quarters to get changed into your swimsuit. While you do, I'll make the sandwiches in the communal kitchen attached to the barracks. We'll eat by the river."

"This is a really bad idea, and sounds way too much like a date."

"It's just a swim." He pulled me closer, his chin rubbing across the top of my head as he sent us zipping away again, so fast.

I bumped down in his cabin and he released me, set my change of clothes on his bed and unstrapped his weapons. He kicked off his boots, unbuckled the belt holding up his jeans and whoa—I whipped around and gave him my back, the swish of denim hitting the floor next. "You are getting far too comfortable around me."

"I'm decent underneath. I already had my swim shorts on

under my jeans. I donned them this morning since I was worried that in capturing and relocating the snakes, you'd end up with another snake bite and demand for another dip in your spa bath. I wanted to be prepared if that happened." He stepped around me, indeed decent and wearing white swim shorts with blue stripes down the sides, his chest bare and his silver snake bands curling around his biceps. He thrust one thumb over his shoulder at the river beyond his window. "I'll meet you outside, with the sandwiches."

"I'm still not sure this is a good idea." I waved my swimsuit at him. "We are going to be scantily dressed."

"I dare you to meet me outside." A wink as he crossed to his bathroom at the end of the cabin and opened the door. Inside, he strode and I followed.

Good grief. So tiny. One step in either direction had me up against a wall, a basic white shower cubicle tucked in one corner, his vanity the other.

He swiped a bar of soap from the vanity cupboard and tucked two plush blue towels under his arm before facing me. "Would you like white, brown, or grainy bread for your sandwiches?"

"I'll have whatever you're having." I loved bread, no matter which way it came. "What's your favorite type of bread?"

"Whatever the camp cook has made. She's a whizz in the camp kitchens and makes the bread fresh each and every morning. See you outside." He shuffled past me, strode out the front door and closed it behind him.

How annoying. He'd brought me here and then dared me to meet him outside and I'd never been able to ignore a dare yet. He was making me a sandwich too, and I couldn't be rude and ignore the meal he'd be offering. I nabbed my clothes from his bed, hung the dress on the back of the bathroom door and stripped out of my dusty and dirty clothes, which I left in a pile in the corner of his poky bathroom. I tugged my white swimsuit on and hiked it out the door.

I hopped down the front steps, my feet sinking into gloriously soft grass. Beautiful.

All remained quiet around the other cabins and men's barracks, only the chirping of birds in the treetops ringing across the clearing.

I jogged around his cabin to the rear where the river weaved through the trees. White water tumbled over a low ledge of gray boulders and rocks before cascading into a wide pool then flowing on downstream and around the bend.

No Sorrell yet. Just me. I sat on one rock among a cluster of rocks rimming the edge and dipped my feet into the cool water. I kicked my legs back and forth, the water deep, crystal clear, and the surface sparkling with sunshine.

"Here we are." Sorrell strode in, towels and soap wedged under one arm, a plate in one hand and a water bottle in the other. He dropped down onto the flat surface of the rock next to me, set everything beside him before holding out a monster sandwich oozing with roast beef, pickles, and cheese, a second monster sandwich already in his other hand.

I slapped my mouth around the sandwich and almost took two of his fingers off with it. "Yummedy-yum-yum," I mumbled as I chewed. "You make great sandwiches."

"Thanks." He chuckled as he passed me the water bottle, then bit into his own sandwich.

"What's it like living here?" I asked as I swigged water.

"I love it."

"Is your brother close?"

"Asar has the cabin next to mine." He cast his gaze to the log cabin right alongside his, one identical in design. "You can see inside his front window. Lock down the image of his place for teleporting so in the future you can 'port directly there."

"I will." A great idea, and I managed to catch enough of the inside of his cabin through the window to manage a future jump.

Another bite and long moan. "Mmm, I swear this is the best sandwich I've ever eaten."

"Do you want me to make you another?" He polished off his and licked his fingertips.

"No, I'm dying to get into the water, and I'd rather float than sink with a heavy belly."

"Come on then." A grin as he pushed to his feet and dove. He disappeared below the surface then popped up in the center of the pool.

He didn't need to tell me twice.

I finished off the last bite and hopped along the embankment of rocks before scrambling across the slick rock ledge. Cool water flowed around my ankles and over my feet. In the center of the ledge, I halted where the water gently swished, my mate treading water only a few feet away.

"Jump." A wave of his hand, his golden hair slicked back from his head and a playful smile on his face. "The water is well over my head here. You won't be able to touch the bottom even if you dive in."

"I can't believe you get to have such a beautiful river and swimming hole right at your back door." I jiggled about, beyond eager to jump in, then unable to hold back a moment longer, I dived and went deep, far enough below the surface to skim underneath his treading feet and pop up behind him. I giggled when I broke for air and squealed as he caught me around the waist and twirled me about in the water. I looped my arms around his neck and held on. "Hope would love it here, particularly with her water skill. She's always dipping and diving about the watering holes after she fills them up from the river."

"Bring her here whenever you'd like." His eyes lit up, the late afternoon sunshine flaring across his high cheeks and strong jaw.

"I wish I could, but that would be a terrible idea." After tonight I'd need to keep my distance from him, and other than checking in with Asar when needed, I'd otherwise steer clear of this magical spot in his beautiful mountains.

I breathed deep of the pine-fresh air then gasped as a deer pranced out of the woods and stepped alongside the bank. Where the water pooled to one side, the deer drank from the lapping edge. "Oh wow."

"We get a lot of deer visiting this river, antelope, and goats as well. Large packs run wild through these woods." He twirled me around until I faced the other side where the cabins and barracks stood. He motioned to three wild turkeys strutting in and out of the trees. "This river draws all manner of wildlife."

"You're so lucky to have all this lush land and these animals. All we get is red dust, vicious snakes, and poisonous spiders." I tugged the violet hairband from my ponytail, slipped it over my wrist and with my hair freed, dunked my head back in the water.

"I didn't realize how lucky we were until today." He leaned in, his nose a mere inch from mine and his wet blond hair curling damply around his shoulders.

"I think we're getting too close." I'd also come to wash up. "I'll grab the soap."

I slipped out of his hold and kicked toward the rocks lining the edge of the pool then when my feet reached the sandy base, I splashed out and pinched his soap. I sat on the rocks as Sorrell floated closer. A quick scrub of my face and arms, my feet too.

Done, I tossed him the soap, which he caught, and dove back under the surface. I didn't want to waste a moment of my time here and I kicked, cutting a fast path underneath the surface toward the other side of the pool. I emerged next to a low overhanging ledge, planted my hands on it and heaved up with a push. I sat on the top of the cool stone, my feet dangling in the water.

Sorrell cleaned himself then set his soap back on the rock.

He swam underneath the water, a wave rippling toward me

and the streak of his white swim shorts easy to see just below the surface, his golden hair too. With a last kick, he burst from the water in front of me, clamped his hands on my knees and arched one brow. "Do you want a race?"

"I can already tell you're faster than me."

"I'll give you a ten second head start." He flashed a smile full of challenge then released me and gestured to the far side of the pool where we'd eaten. "First one to reach the rocks gets to choose their winnings, within reason of course, or are you too wary to race with a protector?"

"I'm wary of no one, and certainly not a protector." A ten second head start would be perfect, and I'd show him I could outswim a protector, or at least I hoped I could. I stood and dove from the top of the ledge. Kicking, I swam hard but only made it halfway before Sorrell drew up alongside me then powered ahead. The cheat. He hadn't given me more than half the allotted time. Laughing, I nabbed his ankles and held on as he plowed onward, his arms alone pulling us both through the water.

Once he made the edge, he hauled himself up onto the rocks and beamed. "I haven't enjoyed a race like that in years."

"Neither have I, and since you cheated, no winnings for you." I held out my hands and he grasped them and lifted me onto the rock beside him. "I'm beat."

"Come and lie on the grass." He bounded to his feet, not exhausted at all, and with our towels in hand, spread them out side by side on the grass before dropping down onto one and sprawling out. With his gaze on the puffy white clouds bobbing across the vivid blue of the sky, he appeared so relaxed.

I laid down beside him, our shoulders touching as I stared at the same beautiful, tranquil sky he did. "I could lie here all day. It's the perfect temperature. Not too hot, and not too cold."

"It gets cooler in the evenings, once the sun has set." He rolled onto his side and played with a lock of my hair. "What's your favorite thing to do?"

"I love dancing in the rain, which hardly ever happens." I rolled and faced him. "What's yours?" I desperately wished to know everything about him, likely the same as he wished with me.

"Before today I would have said swimming in this river, but now I'd have to add to that and say swimming in it with you."

"You shouldn't have said that." I curled one hand into a fist and thumped it against his chest. "No being cute."

"You're the cute one. I'm simply a towering menace who cheats." He waggled a brow. "I only counted to four. You would have beaten me good and proper if I'd gotten all the way to ten."

"You clearly don't like losing a challenge." Which I understood since I hated losing challenges too. As the sun dipped lower toward the horizon and the air cooled, the skies darkened.

"The sun sets quickly in the mountains." He pushed to his feet and extended a hand to me. "You can use my bathroom to change for dinner. It's already six. Is that okay?"

"Sure, sounds perfect." I set my hand in his and he tugged me to my feet, then he scooped the towels and draped them over his arm. He motioned to his cabin, and I walked back inside with him.

While he remained in the main room, I skipped into his bathroom.

I donned my lacy white summer dress, the crisscross straps crossing at the back and the hem swishing about my ankles. I rarely wore my weapons when I dined at night, so I carried them and my bundle of discarded clothes back into his bedroom.

Sorrell sat at the table with his towel wrapped around his waist, but he stood as I emerged, a slow smile breaking out across his face. "I've never had to wait for a girl to use my bathroom before. I kinda liked it."

"I said no being cute." I tapped his nose. "I'm going to head off and see if Hope needs help with dinner. I'll see you when it's time to eat."

"Okay, later." His smile disappeared. "Take care, my mate."

"I always do." I desperately wanted to wrap my arms around his neck and hold him close, only that would be a terribly bad move, so instead I dipped my head and brought forth the image of home. Without another moment's hesitation, I fell away into the dark, my heart falling away into the same darkness as well. My soul got wrenched away from his, the pain spearing sharply through me, a pain I'd have to accept over the days and weeks ahead. I shook my head, the thought almost too much to bear.

Chapter 7

After I tossed my dirty clothes in the hamper and left my weapons beside my bed, I slogged downstairs and joined Hope and Silas in the kitchen. They'd prepped all the food, had baked potatoes cooking in the oven and fresh vegetables steaming on the stovetop. Silas had heated up the frying pan for the steaks and splashed a capful of oil across the base. The steaks sizzled as he placed them down on the hot pan. Next to him, a metal dome covered something on the bench. I motioned to it, asked, "What's under the dome?"

"Silvie made us a dessert and it's a surprise."

"I love Silvie's desserts."

"So do I, but no peeking under that dome." Hope nudged me toward the dining room. "You set the table. We've got the rest covered."

"Okay." Cutlery and glassware on a tray, I moseyed on into the dining room. I swished around the table and set it for four then once done, stepped up to the wide bay window, the moon's golden glow shimmering across the gum trees and the wide-open plains. I released a soft sigh. Such a beautiful sight.

A knock rattled the front door and I called out to Hope, "I'll get that."

I skidded across the midnight blue floor tiles in the foyer, opened the door and grinned as my mate stood there in black leather pants and a pale blue sleeveless shirt, a gaping rip under the front pocket. I poked one finger in it as I looked into his eyes. "I'm curious. Do you own any shirts without rips in them?"

"Nope. I doubt I ever will either." He leaned in and stuck his nose in my hair. "You smell amazing, like fresh water and my soap."

"I wonder how that happened?" Smiling even wider, I gestured toward the dining room. "Head on through. Dinner is almost ready."

"Thanks." He strode into the dining room then halted and eyed the table settings, two on each side of the long oak table.

"Sit wherever you'd like."

"I'll sit next to you." He pulled out two chairs and tipped his head toward one. "Ladies first."

"I thought we already discussed this." I sat where he'd indicated.

"Discussed what?" He frowned as he took his seat, his look of confusion making me smile.

"You're not allowed to be cute, and that includes saying cute things like you wanting to sit next to me."

"Right. Gotcha." He cleared his throat with a frown. "Ah, then you're probably not going to want the gift I got you." Ducking his head, he pulled a violet and golden leafed pansy from his shirt pocket and dropped in on the table between us. "It's from my mother's garden. I couldn't bring a bloodroot flower for fear of poisoning you, and the moment I saw this pansy, the colors reminded me of your violet eyes and your golden hair."

"It's half dead." The poor wilted thing looked like it had been mashed between his fingers while he'd picked it, not that I was going to let him take it back. I nabbed the flower, poured a glass of water and carefully set the pansy floating on the surface. Not too bad. I'd salvaged it at least. I twirled the water with one finger and giggled as the flower swirled and perked up a little.

"This is the prettiest flower anyone has ever given me. Thank you, Sorrell."

"You really like it?"

"I do, and I'll show you exactly how much." I left my chair, collected a pad and pen from the side table which housed the fine crystal and returned to my seat. I penned a quick note while Sorrell leaned over my shoulder to watch.

Dear Mrs. Sona,

You grow beautiful pansies and have a huge, gruff son who is excellent at catching snakes and releasing them. I particularly like the length of his arms, since he can reach down long rabbit holes to fetch unreachable snake eggs for me, even when there aren't any unfortunately there.

Yours sincerely,

Goldwyn Wincrest.

I folded the letter in three, tucked it inside his front shirt pocket and patted it. "I want you to hand this note to your mother for me."

"I can't do that. My mother has no idea I stole the pansy, and she certainly doesn't know I'm mated to you, or that we've released each other. She's going to be furious about that, particularly when she's always wished for my brother and I to find our mates one day."

"Then you've got some serious explaining to do when you see her next." I wriggled in my seat, needing to keep my hands busy or else I'd reach for him and that would be a fatal mistake, one I couldn't make. Instead of making that wrong turn, I poured water from the jug into his glass and nudged it toward him. "Are you thirsty?"

"After spending most of the day in the outback, absolutely." He tipped the glass to his lips, gulped the water down then leaning closer to me, cleared his throat. "So, ah, I've changed my opinion about you today."

"In what way?"

"You might be a Chaser, but you took a great deal of time out of your schedule to catch and relocate snakes which could strike and kill with ease." He settled his arm along the back of my chair, his gaze holding mine captive, his thumb brushing my shoulder. "You understand that even venomous creatures deserve a chance at life, and have taught me that valuable lesson today. I wouldn't have learnt it otherwise."

"Careful, Sorrell, you're showing far too many emotions again and I've been getting bombarded by them today." I filled his glass a second time and gulped the water myself.

"I don't mean to, but around you, I can't seem to help myself." Another brush of his thumb, down my arm to my elbow then back up and over my shoulder.

I tingled everywhere he touched. Goodness. I was so attuned to him and his presence. I shuffled closer, rested a hand on his leather-clad leg and curled my fingers around his inner thigh. "I'll need to find a way to explain why you and your brother are sleeping over in the stables tonight. Hope will wonder otherwise."

"Can't we simply be vague?"

"Ha. With Hope?" He clearly didn't know Hope well enough yet.

"Dinner is served." Hope bustled into the room, two plates in hand and her summery pink dress imprinted with white lilies around the hem, her dress fluttering an inch above her knees. She set the two plates down before us with a flourish. "Please take note, that neither Silas or I burnt the steaks."

"Thank you." I preferred my meat medium rare, but I ate it whatever way it came. Chopped chives, shredded cheddar, and sour cream oozed over the baked potato, while mint swirled through the air from the fresh peas and medley of steamed vegetables. "You two did an awesome job."

"You're welcome," Silas added as he followed with his and Hope's plates, his tan pants neatly pressed and the pointy tip of his wrist dagger glinting under the cuffs of his beige button-down shirt open at his neck. He pulled out a chair for Hope, seated himself and cast his gaze at Sorrell. "I'm glad you came. Hope would be chasing you down by now otherwise."

"I'm glad I'm here too." Sorrell cut through his steak, chewed and moaned his appreciation, then cut another slice and held it out to me. "You want to try some?"

"I've got my own." Although I dipped in and snuck the slice from his fork, and mmm-mmm, I wanted more.

"Look at that. They're sharing food already." Hope popped a kiss on Silas's cheek. "Remember when we first did that?"

"I'll never forget." Silas smoothed a hand around Hope's shoulders as he tucked her right up against him, then proceeded to feed her a slice of his own steak.

"Sorrell brought me a flower." I picked up my water glass and tipped it toward Hope.

"Aww, is that a pansy? How, oh—" Hope frowned as she stared at the tiny violet and golden-leafed flower floating on the surface. "Will it survive?"

"It's looking far more likely now I've got it in water."

"Great, then here's to good food, great company, and the survival of that wee pansy." She picked up her water glass and clinked it to mine.

I set the pansy glass down and poured water into another glass to drink. "By the way," I murmured as I sipped, "Sorrell and Asar are bunking down in the stables tonight. I'm worried about all three mares going into labor at once, so Tawson will have some additional help it that happens." I held my breath as I waited for her answer. *Please, please, please let that excuse fly.*

"Um, okay." A slow nod from Hope, then a conspiratorial wink. "I totally get it. You want Sorrell close, so this is your way of ensuring that."

"It is?"

"Yep, and I think him and Asar staying over is a great idea. It means you're taking my advice to heart, about not giving up on your bond just yet. Silas and I won't even be here tonight anyway, so I can't pitch in to help with the mares should they go into labor. We've got wedding prep with Faith and Davio, then we'll hit the sack at Loveria Castle, although we'll be back first thing in the morning. I promise."

"Great." Relief poured through me as I ate.

"*It appears we got away with that.*" Sorrell's deep voice filled my mind as he scooped peas. "*Asar just telepathed me and asked that I collect him at ten from my quarters. He hasn't been here to the outback before, so he doesn't have the 'porting image.*"

"*I'd like to make a new blood oath with Asar tonight, as soon as I possibly can. Ensuring I maintain accountability with my skill is important to me.*" I chewed, the meat melting in my mouth, the peas minty fresh and the baked potato a smooth and creamy base to the meal. So delicious.

"Sorrell, what do you think about the outback now you've spent some time here?" Hope asked him with inquisitiveness in her tone.

"It's dry, desolate"—Sorrell squeezed my leg under the table, his gaze softening as he eyed me—"yet still brimming with life."

I squeezed his leg in return and he caught my hand and tangled our fingers together.

"Now," he continued to me, "I can see why you picked a fistful of grass from the mountains to bring back. I have more understanding."

"That sounded suspiciously like an apology."

"It was." A smile as he lifted our joined hands to his lips and kissed my fingertips. "My apologies, Princess."

My heart melted, turning into a liquid mess in my chest.

Across the table, Hope softly sighed as she snuggled into Silas's side.

Well, hopefully we'd gotten her off our tails for a bit.

"I believe it's dessert time." Beaming, Hope collected our empty dinner plates and disappeared into the kitchen with Silas. She returned with a flourish and set a decadent cheesecake on the table, Silas following with dessert plates. "This is compliments of Silvie," she said to Sorrell. "It's one of her latest creations. A double chocolate espresso cheesecake with lashings of whipped cream on top."

"I love Silvie and her creations, and that cheesecake looks amazing." He slapped his lips together.

"You can do the honors." Hope handed me the serving knife and took her seat. She refilled our water glasses.

Shaking a little with anticipation, I sliced the cheesecake and plated it, then once I'd served us all, we dove in.

Creamy chocolate with a flavorsome hit of coffee sent my taste-buds dancing across my tongue. I nudged Sorrell's shoulder with mine. "You said you don't drink coffee, and there's coffee in this cheesecake. Can you handle it?"

"I'm not drinking the coffee, I'm eating it." He gobbled his slice down, handling it with perfection. "There's a huge difference."

"There is not, and you also said you don't eat cake. Doesn't cheesecake count as a form of cake?"

"No, and must you remember everything I say?"

"Yes." I giggled as I ate, then after a second slice for each of us, my tummy near to bursting, I leaned back and patted my full belly.

"Are we on dishes?" Sorrell asked with a glance at me as he picked up his empty dessert plate and licked the inside of it.

"Yes, if I can haul myself into the kitchen."

Hope eyed Sorrell licking his plate, then stared at her own empty dish. A smile broke out as she lifted the plate to her face and licked the inside. "Oh, wow." An arch of her brows. "Why have I never done this before?"

Silas chuckled and pushed back his chair before extending a hand to Hope. "C'mon, little duckling, we have places to be, and these two could use some time alone together."

"I thought we agreed the 'little ducking' nickname you keep using has to go." She waved one hand at the jug and the water within swirled and churned as she played with her element. With another wave of her fingers, the water swished free of the jug, arced out and smacked Silas in the face. Water dribbled down his shirtfront and puddled on the floor and Hope grinned while Silas boomed with laughter.

"You said it had to go. I never did." Silas's chest bumped up and down, his laughter making me and Sorrell laugh too. "And I like it when you get mad at me and slap water in my face. It's rather refreshing, particularly out here in the outback. You can do that as often as you like."

"Ugh, even when I try to annoy you, it doesn't work."

"You could never annoy me." He scooped Hope from her feet and sticking his wet face in her neck, shimmered away with her.

"They make a great couple." Sorrell gave his plate one last lick then stood and collected the dirty dishes.

"I would never say this in front of Silas, because it would give him a big head, but I really love the way he loves her." I picked up the glasses and carried them into the kitchen. Carefully, I set my pansy glass on the windowsill overlooking the corral below, then opened the dishwasher and loaded it as Sorrell handed me the plates.

We worked in tandem, tidying the kitchen until it sparkled and once the cleanup was done, I wandered back into the dining room, bundled the used tablecloth and set a clean one down. Sorrell eased in behind me, his big body a wall of heat as I flattened out the odd wrinkle in the ruby-red cloth, his presence comforting me as nothing else ever could.

My heart panged as the time we had left together continued to count down.

He'd done his duty and seen to Hope's wishes, to join us for dinner, and now he had only two chores left, to oversee my meet-and-greet with his brother and to stay the night in the holding room. Come the morning though, he'd be gone and we'd never have the need to see or even speak to each other again. Immense loss and pained grief washed through me. So annoying.

"Hey." Still behind me, he gently settled his hands on my shoulders and turned me around until I faced him. He searched my gaze, clear confusion flaring in his stunning gray-blue eyes. "You've gone quiet. Have I said or done something wrong?"

"No." I leaned in and rested my forehead on his chest, my loss expanding. "It's nothing."

"It looks like something to me."

"Just ignore me."

"I can't." He stroked my back, his touch warm and soft and drat it, I needed more of it.

"Tell me more about your family, Goldie." Whispered words in my ear. "You never speak of your parents."

"Everything you need to know will be recorded in your country's tomes." I gripped his hips, wanting only to cling to him.

"Yeah, there's a lot in there about Donaldo, but not your mother. She died after she gave birth to you. That's all I know." A brush of his chin over the top of my head. "I want to learn more about you and your family. Do you know what I mean?"

I did, particularly when I wished to learn more about him and his family too. I could share a little bit. I cleared my throat. "My parents never expected to have a second child. Carrying Alexo was difficult for my mother, the delivery even more so. The healers said afterward that she'd never bear another child, so when she discovered she was pregnant with me seventeen years later, she got quite the surprise. Or so my father told me. I can only share what he and Alexo have spoken about over the years."

"I want to hear it all." Soft, enticing words.

"Her name was Vespera Iona and my father said she shone like an evening star, although she passed away far too soon at thirty-six." Childhood memories shimmered through me. "Alexo has told me often about our mother's amazing hugs. She gave the best ones, so engulfing and wondrous that he could never forget them. I don't have any personal memories of her though, and will forever be denied them too."

"I'm sorry you never got to know her." He smothered me in an overwhelmingly tender hug, and my heart heaved, my soul tugging ever closer toward his.

I sniffed, the loss of my mother and the soon-to-be loss of my mate rising strongly within me. No. I couldn't cry. I had to remain strong.

I owed it to Sorrell to let him go without any backward glance.

He needed to live his life, and preferably without me.

I pushed away from him and rounded the table to gain some extra distance between us, then I halted at the other end of the room and pressed my hands to my hips. Staring him in the eyes, I muttered, "One can't always miss what they never had, but for some reason I've always missed her."

"One can definitely miss what they never had."

"Hope and I are so close because we understand each other. We were both born without our mothers."

"Hope has her mother now."

"Yes." I breathed a little easier, that knowledge lightening my heart. "I'm incredibly glad Alexo returned to Earth and claimed Kate and Faith, although in truth it was my father who first stood in my brother's way of having the happiness he now holds. Donaldo had no intention of ever accepting Kate since he believed her to be an Earthling."

"Yet now, as we've all learnt, Kate was never an Earthling at all, but a full-blooded Magioling, her parents from the Sol tribe of No-Man's Land." With one hand resting on the hilt of his sword, he stepped around the table. "Do you think your father would ever accept me as your mate? I am a Peacian."

"He's accepted Davio as Faith's mate, and Silas as Hope's, although he was forced into a rather tight corner with them due to the girls' deadly mind-merge skill. They can't survive without their mates. Still, it's not like we're going to pursue our mated bond. You'll be completely safe from him since we've given each other up." I side-stepped around the table as he got closer. "What are you doing?"

"Chasing you." Slowly but surely, he continued that chase.

"I'm the Chaser, not you." I kept moving, light on my feet as I maintained the solid width of the oak tabletop between us. "It's almost ten. You should collect Asar and bring him here so I can speak to him."

"Or we could collect Asar together so we'd have more time with one another." He bounded over the table, slid across the surface on his butt before landing on his feet beside me, a victorious smile on his face as he caught me in his arms. "Hold on tight."

He sent us whizzing away through the dark, stars blazing by and my belly rolling at the sheer speed of his 'port through time and space. I held on for the wild ride until we bumped down within the darkened confines of his cabin.

"Let me light a candle," he murmured as he released me. "Asar won't be far away."

A clop of his boots, a rasp of a match, and a candle flared to life on top of his side table, the light flickering over the two wooden-backed chairs and the walls covered in his weapons.

I crossed to one particularly pretty dirk with a razor-sharp blade and burnished hilt.

"That dirk was gifted to me from my grandfather." He

collected a bedroll from a cupboard then in front of his dresser, opened a drawer and stuffed some clothes into a duffel.

The air stirred and Asar shimmered in, his broad shoulders filling out his padded brown jacket laced over a white tunic, his black leather pants encasing his long legs. He cast his gaze on me, a rather assessing gaze. Sorrell's brother held the same steely-gray eyes as him, including the stunning hint of soft blue at the edge, and with his facial features identical to my mate's in every way, he would always be a firm reminder of what I'd lost.

Expression grim, Asar extended a hand to me, his side sword and daggers donned. "Sorrell has explained everything. I'm aware you need a new guardian and Destroyer."

"You have no issue with that?" I shook his hand.

"No, provided I have your full consent, exactly as you first offered it to my brother. I need a signed letter."

"Of course." Since the letter I'd given Sorrell still sat on his table, I slid the paper from the envelope, picked up the pen from next to the pile of papers and added Asar's name next to Sorrell's. I tucked the paper back inside and handed the letter to Asar. "Will you agree to a blood oath?"

"Absolutely, and this letter can stay here." He set the letter on the table, removed his dagger and sliced his palm, then handed me his weapon.

I accepted it, sliced my own palm and held out my hand.

"I offer you a blood oath." Asar gripped my fingers. "I, Asar Sona, hereby agree to be Goldwyn Wincrest's Destroyer."

Sorrell released an unsettled breath, then motioned for me to continue.

"Everything will be all right." I cast my gaze back to Asar. "I accept your oath, and whatever death you choose for me should I go Dark."

"The law to remove all Chasers is an ancient one and no rules have ever been set in place should a revival of your kind occur, although throughout the centuries our Sona family line of

Destroyers have always maintained justice. My duty, like that of my ancestors before me, will never falter."

"That's all I ask for, that justice be served should I step out of line."

"Chasers always step out of line." Solemn words from Sorrell as he stepped away and clenched the windowsill. He stared out over the river to the forest beyond. "It's just a matter of time until you do."

The tense line of his shoulders drew me toward him and I followed and remained standing quietly at his back. "Sometimes," I whispered, "the snake might strike, but that doesn't mean the snake is a killer. It simply means that is the nature of the snake."

Chapter 8

The weight of the world had descended on my shoulders within the passing of two short hours. As my watch ticked over the midnight hour, I accepted that as my new truth. "Is there anything else either of you two require?"

"I'm all good." Asar flapped out his bedroll at the edge of the wall of stacked hay bales and laid down with his ankles crossed and hands laced behind his head. I'd shown Asar around, Sorrell trailing us, and my new Destroyer now had the 'porting images of all the places on the station I usually visited, including the image of my bedroom.

Sorrell strode to the open doors of the holding room overlooking the corral and leaned one shoulder against the doorjamb. With his gaze moving across the moonlit land beyond the station, he crossed his arms, his silver snake bands gleaming.

"You can shut those doors if you like."

"I'm sleeping in front of them so I can see the night sky." He held out one hand in a silent entreaty for me to join him, and drat it, my stupid feet had me walking across to him. I leaned into his side as he wrapped one arm around me, his next words a rough whisper in my ear, "You're my mate and I haven't even kissed you yet."

"That's a good thing," I whispered right back with a quick glance at Asar, who had a smile on his face and clearly hadn't missed our whispered words at all.

"Don't mind me." Asar lifted his chin and stared at the ceiling, his smile even wider. "You two are mighty close for a mated pair who've released each other. It's hard to miss that."

"Well, we have released each other, and we're not taking that decision back." I returned my gaze to Sorrell and softly sighed. "He's right. We're getting far too close and now he's here, you could leave. There's no reason for you to remain when your brother has things covered."

"I should leave, except I gave you my word I'd remain for tonight." His gaze dipped to my lips, his breath coming harder and faster. "I'm drawn to you in every way."

"As I'm drawn to you." My chest tightened, because deep in my heart, I wanted him to remain.

"I have an idea." He caught my hands and pressed my palms flat to his chest. "A compromise as such."

"What are you doing?"

"I need to align our heartbeats."

"That is a terrible idea." I jerked back, until my shoulders knocked into the wall behind me.

"Then you'll need to stop me, otherwise this is happening." Caging me in, he slapped my hands back on his chest and kept them pinned there with his firm hold. "Aligning our heartbeats will ensure that when you have need of me, I can come to you, immediately. It's the only way we'll both get through this coming separation."

"Try to align our heartbeats, and I'll hurt you." I shoved one knee up, only he met my swift move with one of his own raised knees and blocked me. "Sorrell," I muttered through gritted teeth. "If I have need of you, I can telepath you."

"Not good enough." Anger flared in his eyes, then my hands on his chest heated and my pulse jumped. It leaped a second time before beating steadily in time with his own thumping heartbeat.

Grrr, how annoying. He'd aligned our heartbeats as our mated men did, which meant he'd know every moment when my heart beat too fast or too slow, or when it ceased beating completely. "You shouldn't have done that."

"I disagree." His grip on my hands tightened. "Even though released, I need to be able to feel what you feel, to know when you need me."

"Well feel this." I heaved against his chest and shoved around him. "I'm furious at you."

"Too bad." He stalked me.

"Stay right there." Wagging a finger, I backed into the corridor leading to the stalls. "I need to check on Tawson then I'm heading to bed." One of Saunder's uncles had taken him back to Dralion in the morning, not long after my conversation with Tawson. "Stay away from me, Sorrell. Don't ever come near me again, and I mean it."

"Don't do anything dangerous, and I will." Sparks flared in his eyes.

"I'll do my best." I nabbed the lamp, flicked off the holding room's main light and left the area bathed in moonlight from the open doors as I hurried down the corridor to the large stall housing the three pregnant mares. All held rounded bellies, all due to give birth this week.

I gripped the stall door and with my chin over the top, let out a relieved breath. Tawson was sprawled on a bedroll in the corner, his eyes closed as he slept. Perfect. We had Matilde covered.

No need for me to stick around.

I flashed straight to my bedroom, set the lamp on my nightstand and growled under my breath. No doubt I'd be peeved with Sorrell for some time to come, but that would be a good thing, my anger helping me keep my distance from him.

I stalked into my bathroom, whizzed my toothbrush over my teeth and brushed my hair, the long blond strands snagging in the brush. Once done, I changed into a sunshine-yellow camisole sleep top and matching pajama shorts then dumped myself into bed and fluffed the top sheet over me. Lamp flicked off and sensors flicked on, I growled some more.

"*I still want to kiss you.*" Sorrell's deep voice shimmered inside my head.

"*That's never happening, so get over it.*"

"*I like it when you get all feisty with me, and from where I'm lying, your balcony door is in my direct line of sight. Do you remember me saying that I find a tough and dangerous woman, sexy?*"

"*Yeah, and that Belle could have tamed your hardened heart with no issue at all.*" I thumped my pillow and nestled my head deeper into it. "*Perhaps you should think about dating another empath like her.*"

"*There's no one else like Belle.*" Fondness tinged his tone.

"*Grrreat.*" I closed our link and blocked it. I didn't want to hear about how fond he was of Belle, not when I actually liked Belle and didn't want to have to slit her throat the next time we saw each other. Huh, and yeah, I was jealous. I couldn't miss that emotion stirring within me, but it was all his fault for being so annoyingly cute all the time. He'd picked me a flippin' pansy today. What had he been thinking?

With the air humid and sticky, I tried to find a position where I could fall asleep, only I missed Sorrell badly. I wanted my mate back, the man who was gruff and huge, excellent at catching snakes and releasing them, and could make awesome sandwiches. Not to mention, he could annoy me without even being around. Yeah, I wanted his arms wrapped around me, all night and every night to come. Stupid, silly, idiotic, mated bond.

A dingo howled somewhere far in the distance, its call being answered by another dingo somewhere closer by. Whoa.

I shoved up onto my elbows in bed. Of course, it wasn't unusual for dingoes to howl at night, but my vision of foreboding had included the howling of two dingoes, one right after the other. I activated my link with Tawson. *"Hey, how's everything going with Matilde?"*

"She's just gone down onto her side and is jerking about. She's in labor, which has happened really quick. Can you come?"

"I'm on my way." I hit the switch and turned the sensors off, tugged on my boots and heck, I didn't have time to get dressed. These pajamas would have to do.

I 'ported straight to Matilde's stall, a lamp on the wall illuminating the mare and Tawson at her rear, the other two horses resting to the side. Gee, poor Matilde. She had two foal legs out, and was squeezing and pushing to birth her baby. Fast labors could be painful for the mothers with their abrupt speed. I dropped onto my knees next to Tawson. "What do you need me to do?"

"The sac is still intact and her foal is coming hard and fast. I'd say our girl has this under control, except she could use a little hand. I'll break the sac while you check the foal's head when it comes out." He slit the sac with his dagger, clasped the foal's front legs and gently pulled.

The mare snorted and pushed.

"C'mon, Matilde. Sweet girl, keep pushing." I kept my tone encouraging, then with another push from Matilde, the foal's head emerged. I cleared the sac away from it, while Tawson kept ahold of the foal's front legs. "One more push, sweetie, and your baby will be here."

Matilde's belly contracted, and with a harsh snort and heave from her, Tawson pulled and the foal plopped out. "We have another girl." A beaming grin from Tawson.

Happiness surged through me as I swept the rest of the sac free from around the foal's rear legs, then tipped the wee one's head up and checked its mouth remained clear. Matilde heaved to her feet as if she hadn't just given birth, dipped her head and nudged her foal to get her little one moving as quickly as possible. The foal wobbled as she got her front legs bent at her elbows and rear legs bent at her knees.

With the foal here, I opened my link with Sorrell. *"Hey, Matilde just had her foal. Everything happened really fast. How's everything in the holding room?"*

"Stay right where you are." A crash ricocheted and the harsh hit of steel on steel clanged down the passageway.

No, no, no.

"I have to go." I eyed Tawson. "Remain here with Matilde and her foal. That's a direct order which must be followed." I didn't want him anywhere near the holding room, or to find out what I truly was. I had to keep my Chaser status a secret.

"Of course." An uncertain nod, but Tawson had never gone against a direct order and I didn't expect him to now.

"Sorrell!" I took off at a run, one hand on the wall to guide me through the dark. "Sorrell!"

"Stay back," he yelled.

A scuffle, then a grunt and thump.

I reached the main holding room where only a patch of moonlight shimmered through the open doors. Metal glinted, a dagger flying from a cloaked figure within one darkened corner right toward Asar. Sorrell dived in front of his brother and bellowed as the blade embedded deep into his belly. He thumped to the floor, taking Asar with him, his sword clattering against the floorboards.

I skidded in beside them both.

Blood ran in a river of red as Sorrell lay face-down over his brother.

I heaved and Asar moaned as I freed him.

The hairs on my arms rose as I searched the shadows, the cloaked figure moving deeper into them. So much blood, and Sorrell's breath rattled in his chest.

"I'm right here." I seized his face. "Don't leave me,

Sorrell."

I ripped his bloodied shirt open, gripped the gaping wound and cried out to our warrior healer. *"Nicolas, I need you now. The stables at Wincrest Station. Sorrell Sona is badly wounded."*

"I'm on my way."

"Asar, are you all right?" I leaned over Sorrell and grabbed Asar's arm.

"Yeah." He squeezed his eyes shut then opened them. "I got knocked out for a second. Whatever's in here is evil and not entirely human." He heaved to his feet, muttered, "Stay with my brother."

"I won't leave his side."

Asar slid his metal mallet free from his hip, his sword from the other. He advanced toward the shadowed corner. "What the hell are you?" he blasted the shadowed form.

"I am the Darkness." An eerie answer and the air moved as the cloaked figure floated forward. A vicious laugh welled from whatever it was, red eyes glowing within the blackened hood.

With a vicious war cry, Asar slammed his metal mallet into it and the evil thing snagged the mallet with blackened fingertips and heaved it back.

Asar ducked, his mallet crashing into the wall above his head.

The evil thing's eyes glowed a brighter red then it turned and glared at me. "I shall return for you, Chaser. You're of dual blood, which I will take for myself."

"I'm not going anywhere with you." I leaned over Sorrell and scooped his sword from the floor.

Sorrell snagged my hand, blood dribbling from one corner of his mouth, his eyes dazed as he shook his head. "You can't touch whatever that thing is. Kill it, and Asar has to kill you. Only a Destroyer can take it down. Don't break the rules."

Another evil laugh, the Darkness dissolving into an inky mist and streaming out the door. "You shall be mine, Chaser," it cackled as it flew higher. "All mine."

"Damn it. Get back here." Asar chased after it, slashing his sword through the mist which disintegrated and vanished on the wind.

"Asar, Nicolas is on his way. I need your help." I gripped the edges of Sorrell's wound, his eyes sliding shut and head slumping to the side.

"I'm coming." He jogged back to me and knelt at my side, clear anguish slashing his face and a guttural groan tearing from him as he eyed his brother. "That thing is unkillable."

"I won't let it hurt either you or Sorrell again." I'd make sure of it. How ever I had to, no matter Sorrell's decree only a Destroyer could take it down.

"We're here." The air stirred and Nicolas 'ported in with Belle at his side.

Belle slid to her knees next to me and gently lifted Sorrell's head into her lap. More blood dribbled from his mouth and trickled across her jeans.

"Nicolas, you need to hurry." How could I have dragged my own mate into my problems? "This is all my fault," I whispered raggedly to Nicolas. "You have to heal him."

"How did he get hurt?" A light radiated in a gentle glow all around Nicolas as he crouched over Sorrell.

"By something we've never seen before," Asar answered. "It remained cloaked in black and had no form. It called itself the Darkness, and when I struck it with a killing blow from my mallet, it simply dissolved into a black mist and streamed away."

"It's after me. It knew I was a Chaser." I couldn't halt the words from pouring forth.

"You're a Chaser?" A gasp as Belle's eyes went wide. "But Chasers have been extinct from our world for centuries. There aren't even any Chasers in your Wincrest line, and I should know. Hope and I have been comparing our ancient tomes of late."

"I'm definitely a Chaser. I've even had the dreams of foreboding, and right now I want to kill whatever that Darkness is." I wanted to twist its head off with my bare hands then slice and dice it.

"You need to let me kill it." Asar rested a hand on my arm. "Those are the rules which govern your kind. Stick to them."

"Goldie?" Sorrell stirred with a raspy mutter of my name then went quiet again.

"His stomach is slit open and his colon has been nicked." Nicolas swept his hands over Sorrell's belly, his healing-heat increasing in strength and blasting out as he focused his energy on repairing Sorrell's wound. "His spleen has been ruptured and the blood pouring from him is coming directly from that wound. I've got this though." Nicolas's aura glowed brighter as he glanced at me. "As I'm healing him, I can also feel the mated bond pulsing between the two of you. It's strong, incredibly strong. He's aligned your heartbeats. That I can definitely sense."

"I knew it." A gasp from Belle. "You two are a mated pair."

"Yes, but it's a bond we haven't accepted." I shook my head at her. "We're a terrible match, what with me being a Chaser and all." Hot tears coursed down my cheeks, and I leaned my forehead against Sorrell's forehead. "Would you wake up already."

Asar wrapped an arm around my shoulders. "Try speaking mind-to-mind with him. I've already given him a telepathic blasting, but he's ignoring me."

"I'll try." I touched Sorrell's mind along our link. *"Nicolas is working on you, and Asar and Belle are here too. Please, please, don't leave me. I need you."*

Nicolas ran his hands over Sorrell's belly, his golden glow flaring with immense strength, and Sorrell jerked. "I've sealed his spleen and fixed the nick to his colon. I'm working on the gaping slice to his stomach now."

"Did you hear me, Sorrell? Don't you dare leave me to deal with this Darkness-thingy all on my own. I forbid it." I didn't want him anywhere near that thing again, but I was desperate to invoke his protective instincts, and those words would surely work.

"I would never leave you or my brother." Gruff, croaky, heart-twisting words. They echoed through my mind.

"Then open your blasted eyes."

"I'm trying." He groaned and slowly blinked his eyes open, then lifted one hand and caught Asar's hand as Asar reached out to him. "What did I miss?"

"I'll run you through it all." Asar held Sorrell's hand in his fisted hold. "That thing called itself the Darkness and unfortunately, it's unkillable. My mallet went right through it, then it transformed into a mist and streamed away. It's after your girl, said it will return for her, that she's of dual blood, which he wants to take for himself."

"What dual blood?" Sorrell stared at me.

"I've no idea what that thing meant when he said that."

"You jumped in front of me, Sorrell." A hiss from Asar. "I could have ducked that dagger in time."

"I couldn't risk you getting hit, not when it's your job to keep my mate safe." Sorrell released Asar then wrapped his hand around my nape, his fingers so sweetly warm on my skin. "Come closer. Your heart is beating all out of sync and I need to help correct it."

"The healing is complete." Nicolas's golden glow slowly dimmed, Sorrell's skin having sealed together, a pale pink line now all that showed. "Sorrell, you'll have to take it easy for the next twelve to twenty-four hours. Your middle will be tender and your balance off."

"I'll take it easy." Sorrell tipped his head back in Belle's lap and smiled at her. "Fancy seeing you here."

"Yeah, fancy that." Belle popped a kiss on his forehead,

clear relief washing across her face, just as I didn't doubt it washed over mine too. "Sorrell, we know Goldie's a Chaser, and we'll be here to help you and Asar guard and watch over her."

"You have my thanks, Belle." Sorrell returned his gaze to me, his fingers kneading firmer around my neck. "I told you to come closer."

"I'm close enough." Frustration and worry churned in my gut.

"Since you're telling your mate off, I'd say you've healed enough to move." Nicolas gripped Sorrell's arms and tugged him into a seated position, then took his hands and pulled him to his feet.

Sorrell swayed, but remained standing, then he pulled me into his arms. Rubbing his chin over the top of my head, he stroked my back. "Time to get your heart beating right again."

"That might take all night."

"I'm in for the long haul."

No, I couldn't allow that, except he had a fiercely determined look on his face that currently said he'd be getting his way.

Chapter 9

"Goldie, wake up." Sorrell's heavenly voice, albeit a raspy growl, stirred me from my slumber as he held me close in my bed. Where he shouldn't be, but where I'd been unable to turn him away from last night after the attack by the unkillable thing.

With my cheek pressed to his bare chest, I blinked my eyes open then closed them again as the dawn sun blazed through the glass balcony slider. Last night, after all that had happened, Asar had chosen to bed down in the bedroom across the hallway, while Sorrell had promptly walked into my bedroom holding his tender belly and told his brother he'd be sleeping with me. He'd then shrugged out of his bloodied shirt, tossed it into my bathroom waste bin, cleaned the blood from his chest and hauled me into bed with him.

Raising a complaint hadn't been possible.

"Are you awake yet?" Another growl from my very determined mate.

"You are not a morning person." I cuddled closer. "How's your middle feel?"

"A little bruised, but nothing I can't handle." He stuck his nose in my hair and breathed deep. "I can't stop wondering what the Darkness meant when he spoke of your dual blood."

"That goes for two of us." Although I intended on discovering exactly what he meant as soon as I could.

"Things have changed since last night. I'm glad Belle and Nicolas are now aware of what's going on." He squeezed me tight. "We're not just searching for a killer, but something far worse. Asar and I are going to need all the help we can get to locate and deal with this thing."

"You and Asar?" I sat up with a fierce frown. "Your duty to me came to an end last night. You aren't even supposed to still be here. It's morning, and we had an agreement. I get to slice your head off."

"I can't leave you now, and nothing you say will make me leave you either, not when you need me." He eased up, pressed his back to the headboard then seized me around the waist and lifted me fully into his lap. "I truly need to kiss you, and that need is worse than it was last night."

"Kissing is dangerous."

"You love danger."

"They say Chasers begin to lose their minds once their skill comes into being, that they can no longer trust either themselves or their fragmented thoughts any longer, and that when that happens, they're doomed. Perhaps I'm already losing my mind. I must be since I allowed you to sleep in my bed yet again."

"Your mind is perfectly intact." He cupped my face in his hands, his thumbs gently brushing back and forth across my cheeks. "I still want to kiss you."

"We just agreed that would be dangerous." I slapped one hand over his mouth. "No kissing is permitted."

He pried my fingers away. "I should never have released you."

"Sorrell, no. Don't say that."

"Even though we've released each other, our bond grows stronger with each hour we're together. I can't deny it any longer, and I don't wish to." The steely-gray of his eyes got steelier.

"You're not thinking clearly."

"You're right. I should have kissed you already."

"Wait, wait, wait!"

"No, no, no!" He captured my hands, pressed a kiss to my forehead, then each cheek. "The mated bond holds a powerful foundation for those who are soul-bound, and it's a bond which my parents hold, one of absolute depth and devotion. I finally understand now why any separation between them is so difficult. I can't stand it myself when I'm separated from you, so moving forward, we stick together."

"I'm an assassin who will one day wish to kill, and rather ruthlessly. You can't change who I am, or what will become of me."

"You can't even kill a venomous snake. In fact, I've only ever seen you taking absolute care of everything and everyone around you. I desire only you, Goldie." He toppled me back onto the mattress and eased in over top of me. "Before I kiss you the way I've been longing to, I have something very important I need to say."

"I'm not listening to a word that comes out of your mouth."

"Yes, you are." He smiled, cute dimples indenting each side of his mouth. "I, Sorrell Sona of Peacio, hereby revoke my decision to release Goldwyn Wincrest of Dralion. She is my mate, today, tomorrow, and for all time to come."

"You have clearly gone mad." I tried to keep a stern expression on my face, except my heart soared and my soul lifted toward his at the sweetest words I'd ever heard.

"Now it's your turn," he whispered, his mouth a mere inch from mine.

Oh goodness. I desperately wanted this stolen moment in time with him, so I hooked my hands around his neck and drew his mouth to mine. I kissed him and got completely and utterly lost. We shared breath, our hearts beating in time.

Then he kissed me deeper, or I should say devoured me, and I clung to him.

I sunk into his delicious hold with a soft murmur of need escaping me.

Oh boy. I should be pushing him away, not pulling him closer.

That's right. I needed to reaffirm some space.

I eased back a touch, traced a finger over his full bottom lip and tried to instill my usually good sense back into place.

"I'm waiting," he murmured, the hope in his eyes tearing at me.

"I can't revoke my decision to release you, no matter how much I might want to. There's an evil thing after me, and all I want to do is keep you safe."

"I'm not letting you tackle the Darkness on your own." He sucked my trailing finger into his mouth, and my heart lurched and skipped a beat. He jerked and thumped his chest. "Are you all right?"

"No." I stretched out more fully underneath him, his weight so delicious, and grrr, I clearly wasn't thinking straight. I needed to make him leave. I poked him in the chest. "You need to go."

"I need to stay." He caught my finger and kissed the tip.

"Stop being so cute. Either you leave, or I will leave."

"Try and escape me now, and we'll be having words." He touched his nose to my nose, his lips lifting in a soft smile. "How about we just get back to kissing since at least when our lips are busy, we're not arguing?"

"Kissing is off the agenda. I need to get up and get moving. I wouldn't mind a bath. I don't think I got all your blood off me last night." Which he never should have shed in the first place.

"If you're having a bath then so am I. Splashing about with you, in a tub or a river, is rather addictive." He scooped me from the bed, his lips softly touching mine as he carried me into my bathroom. Gently, he set my feet down on the white-tiled floor, plugged the hole and lifted the gold lever over the sunken tub. He added a splash of bubble bath and a mass of vanilla scented bubbles foamed.

"I shouldn't be encouraging you." Yet I couldn't help myself from slinging my feet over the edge. In my sleep top and pajama shorts, I sloshed into the water.

"Water is a precious commodity in the outback. We need to do our bit by saving it where we can." He stepped into the bath in his leather pants, rolled in beside me and sent the bubbles rising higher, then he planted delicious kisses all over my nose and cheeks, the heated look he sent me quickly curling my toes.

I wrapped my arms around his neck and wanted to drown in his beautiful gaze.

Dozens of kisses later, I almost did.

Not good.

Kissing him was dangerous.

I let go of him and got busy cleaning myself.

I scrubbed the blood from my pajamas with soap, then bounded out and nabbed a towel.

Distance. We needed lots of distance.

I hiked it into my dressing room, selected my favorite pair of washed-out blue jeans and teamed them with a violet V-necked tee which matched my violet eyes to perfection. I pulled on socks and stuffed my feet into tan ankle-length boots, strapped my weapons on and armed myself well for the day ahead. When I stepped into my bedroom, I halted as Sorrell shimmered in.

He'd returned from somewhere, likely home since he was now dressed in dry clothes. He wore black jeans and a short-sleeved dove-gray shirt, which had probably been far darker at some point in time since splotches of black showed here and there. With his silver snake bands coiled around his muscled biceps and his weapons donned, he appeared every inch the fierce Destroyer he was.

"You shouldn't be here." I marched into my bathroom, plucked my brush from the vanity drawer and pulled it through my damp hair. "We can't remain together."

"I disagree. Nothing else makes sense, other than that we remain together." From behind me—his gaze moving over mine in the mirror and his hands planted on the counter either side of my body—he hemmed me completely in, his broad chest pressed to my back and his head dipping to my neck. He brushed his lips back and forth over the sensitive skin where my pulse beat. "I love kissing you."

"Sorrell Sona."

"I'm not letting you go again, Princess." He seized my hips, turned me around and kissed the tip of my nose. "I returned home to change and to collect something special, a gift for you."

"I'm not accepting any gifts, particularly from you."

"Yes, you are, and ah, don't freak out." He reached into his back pocket and stilled. "Do you remember when we talked about my snake bands?"

"Yes." My chest tightened.

"I told you how my father gifted me with my bands, and that my mother gifted me with a smaller and identical version of the same ones. But what I didn't tell you is that she asked me to gift those bands to the woman I would one day be mated to, and I've held onto them ever since. Now I know that woman is you, and it's time for me to pass along my mother's gift."

"I'm certainly not accepting any family heirlooms from you."

"They're inscribed with the same sayings that are etched into mine." He caught my right hand and threaded one of the beautiful silver snake bands up my arm and settled it in place over my bicep. "This one says, *Our greatest battles are those with ourselves*. Always keep those words in mind." Then he slipped the other band over my left hand and settled it high to match the placing of the first. "While this one says—"

"*Only you can control your own happiness*, I recited as I read the words out loud." My heart pounded, tears misting my gaze at the beautiful gift he'd given me. Gently, I stroked one finger along the fine silver, the inscriptions on both bands touching my heart.

"Will you accept this gift?" he asked, his gaze intense.

"I'll wear them for today, but tomorrow, I'm handing them right back." The silver warmed against my skin, as if they should've always been mine.

"They belong to you. Can't you sense it?"

"No."

"Liar." He tapped my nose. "I can sense any lies you speak through our mated bond."

"Being mated to me is hazardous to your health."

"I'm a protector. I can hazard anything you throw at me."

"You're a lunatic."

"Sorrell?" A knock rattled my bedroom door, Asar's deep voice floating through.

"I'll go and update Asar on my decision to revoke my release of you. He needs to know." He brushed a kiss across my lips and disappeared into my bedroom.

"*Goldie?*" Hope's voice bounced around inside my head, her tone holding a very definite growl. "*I'm at Loveria Castle in Silvie's kitchen and she and Faith are whipping up pancakes, or I should say Silvie's whipping them up and Faith has her nose deep in the cream bowl and is slurping it down. Belle's here too and she's just informed us all about what happened last night. You've got a lot of explaining to do, and pronto. Come and join us girls for breakfast. That wasn't a request either.*"

"*Ooo-kay.*" No more hiding the truth from my loved ones any longer. No more dragging Sorrell around with me too, not if I could help it. "*I'm on my way.*"

I snuck a peek out my bathroom door. Sorrell and Asar stood speaking, both engrossed in their current conversation about me. Good. I could sneak away.

I 'ported through a whirlwind of dark to Loveria Castle and

arrived in Silvie's cozy kitchen with its gleaming bright red countertop and matching red kitchen cabinets trimmed with white. Over the stainless-steel sink, a wide window overlooked a green garden flourishing with Silvie's favorite herbs. Silvie stood at the stovetop, an apron fastened over her white cargo pants, her bright yellow shirt popping with color underneath, her red-gold hair swaying about her shoulders and her brow arched at me.

Like a pro, she tossed a sizzling pancake, which splattered perfectly in the center of the pan on the uncooked side. "Well, well," she murmured. "The secretive one is here, the first Chaser to grace our world in centuries. Actually, I never would have guessed that. You might be a warrior with the battle skill, but deep inside your heart you're far too level-minded to be an assassin. I can only see you fighting a fair fight with any would be murderer you saw in your dreams of foreboding, never killing anyone outright."

"I'm truly sorry for the secrecy, and unfortunately I will one day kill." Which made my stomach churn with unease. "Those with my assassin ability always do. History has decreed what I will be."

"Yeah, there is that too. Ridiculously, icky history." She flipped the cooked pancake onto a platter, rounded the kitchen bench and squeezed me tight. "Except we all know your heart and we're gonna keep you from any possible kill. Mark my words. None of us girls will ever let you stray down the wrong road. We're tenacious like that. You will be the first Chaser who never goes Dark. You'll live a long life, with us annoying you every step of the way."

"I'd agree with the annoying part, and talking about the girls. Where are they?" I nibbled on my thumb nail.

"Faith, Hope, and Belle are setting the table. We've got your back, all of us." Another squeeze then she returned to her hot pan and swirled more pancake batter. She checked the oven next, opening the glass door. Steam plumed as she poked a fork into a ham and cheese breakfast casserole, one of my favorite breakfast meals which she made. So hearty and delicious.

"There's the secretive one." Grim-faced, Hope marched through the swing door into the dining room, her tan outback riding boots laced to her knees and her violet gaze narrowed on me.

"I can explain." I held up both hands.

"No explanation is needed," Hope muttered as she swamped me in her arms, her blond hair pulled into a braid with wispy strands of hair loose at the sides. "I love you so much and will never lose you to some ugly, unkillable, red-eyed, evil thing. Belle gave us the description, and the horror story of what happened. I'm so sorry you felt the need to keep your new skill a secret from us all."

"Yeah, we're not going to let that Darkness thingy take you away from us." Faith, hot on Hope's heels, charged into our hug and mushed her cheek against my cheek, her blue swing-top loose over her denim shorts. With a soft sigh, she squeezed us both even tighter. "Mmm, I love squishy cuddles and I can't get enough of them right now. The babies are wriggling about, all happy and excited about this hug too."

"It's our Wincrest blood," I mumbled into her hair. "It's strong and will be calling to them through our familial blood-bond." Which was another reason why my need to protect Hope and Faith from all my problems still surged strongly through me. I wanted to kill the Darkness, to wring its neck, and to make sure it got nowhere near my loved ones. If they got hurt, it would be all my fault and that would kill me.

"Hey." Faith gripped my shoulder. "We're all in this together. You can't shake us now. The entire leading eight and your two fearsome Destroyers will be right by your side the entire way."

"Aww, I'm missing out on hugs." Belle swept into the room

in her hot pink blouse and white summery skirt, silver loops dangling from her ears. She joined in our hug, murmured in my ear, "I had an excellent idea this morning. You and I should hit the library after breakfast, and we'll see if we can find out more about the Darkness that's after you. There might be something within the tomes which could lead us in the right direction, so we can find whatever it is and destroy it."

"I wouldn't mind some help in discovering what the Darkness is." Not in destroying it though. That I wanted to handle on my own. I hugged Belle harder, until she squeaked and giggled. Empaths loved lots of crushing hugs.

"I'm so glad you and Sorrell have found each other." Belle rubbed my back.

"I'm not. It sucks being mated to him. He's a protector, and a terribly stubborn one at that. All I want to do is protect him, to keep him out of my business and at a safe distance."

"Yeah, and he'll be feeling just as overprotective of you, as you are of him. His need to ensure your care will be rising strongly within him." Belle slid out a bar stool from under the kitchen counter and perched on it. "That's the way of the mated bond, I'm afraid."

"*Goldie?*" A growling mutter in my head. "*Where. Are. You?*"

"And speaking of that stubborn protector." I tapped my head. "He's asking me right now where I am. I need some advice on how to get around him. We might be mated, but we released each other and now he's gone and revoked his release and is waiting on me to do the same. Chasers don't live long and I doubt I'll be any different, not if my kind's history is anything to go by."

"No one is more stubborn than Davio, so I can give you some advice if you like." Faith checked her watch. "Here's how you can grab a few extra minutes to yourself when you need it."

"Spill." I leaned forward, eager to hear more.

"Tell Sorrell you're in the indoor training room at Loveria Castle. Davio and Nicolas are running a session there together, and Sorrell will surely get sidetracked by them when he pops by to find you. It's all about distract, distract, distract."

"If I tell Sorrell I'm in the training room and I'm not, he'll pick up on that lie."

"Oh, yeah, mated bond. He will." A knowing nod from Faith, then a lift of her brow. "I have an idea. I'll tell him for you. Close your link and I'll fire one up with him."

I did, without hesitation, and Faith gave me a thumps-up as she connected with Sorrell. Thirty seconds later, she grinned. "Okay, your mate is headed to the indoor training room right now."

"You are so full of wisdom, oh wise one." I struck a bow. "I am forever in your debt."

"I'll always be forever in yours too, Goldie." Faith perched on the breakfast bar stool next to Belle and picked up the bottle of maple syrup. With her gaze on me, she flicked the cap and squirted some straight into her mouth, then around her mouthful mumbled, "Since the day we met, you've been on my side. Hope and I will do anything and everything we can to find out more about the Darkness and ensure your protection. While you and Belle check out the tomes here, Hope and I will do a little investigating back in Dralion."

"If you're talking about investigating the tomes at the palace, then I know those well. I've never seen anything about the Darkness within them. Nothing rings a bell at all." Peacio's tomes though were foreign to me, and I definitely wished to scour those.

"I'm not talking about the tomes in Dralion, but rather speaking to some of the Destroyers within our country to see what information they might hold about Chasers. Sometimes you've gotta go to the source, not that you can do that right now, not when we need to keep the fact you're a Chaser under-wraps.

I doubt our world is ready yet to learn that the assassin skill has returned." Another squirt of syrup, which Faith chased up with a finger swipe of cream from the cream bowl.

"That's not a bad idea, speaking to some of the Destroyers." I had steered clear of Dralion's Destroyers, but Faith and Hope could approach them as I couldn't.

"Excellent. We have a solid plan for the day." Faith licked her lips. "A sweet, solid plan."

"Speaking of sweet, you should drink some water with all that sweet syrup and cream." Belle nabbed a napkin from the tray holding the toppings for the pancakes and wiped a smear of cream from Faith's cheek. "Those babies will be getting drunk on all the sugar you've consumed otherwise."

"My babies like sugar."

"You mean you like sugar." An arch of Belle's brow.

"No, I looove sugar, so between the three of us, with my love of it and their like of it, I'm having to triple my sugar intake every day." Faith plucked a strawberry and waved it in front of Belle's nose. "That's not an easy feat by the way, especially when I need something sour after all that sweet stuff."

"It sure looks like you're managing fine to me." Silvie stacked another cooked pancake on top of the mound of pancakes then handed the platter to me. "Pop this on the table. I'm starving now after watching the pregnant one eating all the toppings." To Belle, Silvie said, "Can you take the breakfast casserole out of the oven?"

"Absolutely. I'm on it." Belle stuffed oven mitts on, pulled out the casserole and closed the oven with a knock of her hip against the glass door.

"I've got the maple syrup and cream." Faith, syrup bottle clutched to her chest and bowl of cream firm in her other hand, slid from her stool and held the swing door into the dining room open.

Belle passed through with the steaming dish of ham and

cheese, and I followed with the pancakes, while Hope brought up the rear with the tray of diced fresh fruits, blackberries, bananas, and plump strawberries.

I set the platter down in the center of the dining table covered with a lacy white tablecloth. Cutlery and glasses sparkled, as did the chandelier overhead, the sun shining through the wide window overlooking the inner courtyard and twin-towered gatehouse standing three-stories high.

"Someone is in trouble," Davio muttered as he strode through the hallway door in his black battle leathers, his gaze on me. "That would be you, Wincrest. You've upset one of my protectors by disappearing on him."

Nicolas powered in after Davio, then called out over his shoulder, "Your mate is in here, Sorrell."

Pounding footsteps and Sorrell stepped in and bore down on me.

"Distract, distract, distract," Faith muttered madly from across the table. "How ever you possibly can."

"Right. I've got this."

"So have I," Sorrell grumbled as he dipped me back and planted his lips on mine. He kissed me and oh wow, he sure showed his anger in a delicious way.

"Silvie made pancakes," I murmured against his lips. "Are you hungry?"

"I'm famished." Another grumble and wicked kiss.

Chapter 10

Sorrell pulled out a chair and gestured for me to sit.

I perched on the edge and forked a pancake from the platter onto my plate, while Belle served the casserole and placed a dish next to each of us.

Everyone else took their seats too, even Nicolas who lifted Belle from her seat when she sat and stole a lip-smacking kiss as he settled her in his lap.

Davio snuck the maple syrup from Faith and waved it teasingly in front of her nose before squirting some straight into his mouth.

"Hey, that syrup is all mine." She grasped his face in her hands and captured his mouth with a dreamy sigh and nibbling kiss. "You're such a tease."

"Hey, everyone." Guy shouldered through the door with his Stetson in his hand and riding boots covered in red dust, his nose wafting through the air as he sailed right across to Silvie seated at the end of the table. He pulled out the chair next to hers, dug one fork into his casserole and moaned his approval as he kissed her heartily on the lips. "I love my hot-headed one."

"I love you too." Silvie glowed, her face all pink and flushed as she kissed Guy right back.

Silas marched into the room with loose hay poking out of his red-gold curls, his side sword swaying and the hem of his black and white checked outback shirt loose over his jeans. "I heard we have a Chaser in our midst."

"Yeah, but a wonderful and loving Chaser." Hope plucked the straw out. "Have you been rolling about in the hay?"

"I was cleaning out one of the stalls and accidentally poked Tawson in the butt with the pitchfork. We ended up having a bit of a hay fight, but I'm pretty sure I won." Lips kicked up, he cast his gaze to me. "Matilde's foal is already tackling the newborn run. It's the sweetest thing to see."

"That's great to know." I couldn't wait to see Matilde and her foal.

"I'm glad you got Saunder away from the station before that evil thing came." Silas dug into his ham and cheese casserole and slapped his lips together with delight. A wink at Silvie. "Sis, this is delicious. I love you."

"Everyone loves—" Silvie jumped as Guy nipped her neck. "Hey, I'm not your breakfast."

"But you're just as tasty." Another nip and Silvie sighed and snuggled into his side.

Across the table, Faith and Hope spoke quietly to each other, their foreheads furrowed and clear worry darkening their violet eyes. I leaned across and grasped both their hands. "Hey, I'll be fine."

Hope squeezed my fingers in return. "We've just been talking about Donaldo. You can't keep him or Alexo in the dark for much longer. They both need to know what's going on."

"I'll tell them in the next couple of days. I've barely told you guys." I needed a little more time before I broke the terrible news to them. I rested a hand on Sorrell's leg as I ate, the need to touch him strong, his presence annoyingly comforting.

Sorrell slid one hand under my hair and smoothed around my neck. He dipped in, touched his lips to mine and such warmth spread through me. "We'll tell your father and brother when you're ready, and not a moment before."

Davio tipped up his chin as he eyed me, his brown hair wisped with gold brushing his shoulders. "I won't speak to Carlisio or my father until after you've informed your family. It wouldn't be right for me to do so otherwise."

"I'd appreciate that." I also understood why Davio couldn't keep my Chaser status to himself, not when the leading eight of our world had agreed to keep both kings of our world informed about any and all things.

I ate another bite as conversation resumed around the table, the discussion moving from me and settling on the double wedding. Normal conversation, which I truly needed. It made me feel normal for a moment in time.

After we all finished eating, Guy pushed to his feet. He and Silas both needed to return to the station and they flashed away after saying a quick goodbye.

Hope and Faith came around the table and hugged me, both of them promising to keep me updated on anything they uncovered with the Destroyers they intended on speaking to within Dralion. I gave them the same promise in return, that whatever Belle and I uncovered, we'd share with them as soon as possible.

"I need to get back on duty." Nicolas tucked his chair in and gave Belle a nuzzling kiss before shimmering away, our warrior healer too returning to Dralion where he was needed.

"Let's hit the library now." Belle grasped my hand and tugged me to my feet. "We've got a lot to cover in working through the tomes."

"I'm eager to make a start." Beyond eager.

I strode down the hallway with Belle and Sorrell.

We entered the library through wide double oak doors and I blew out a long breath. Rich mahogany shelves overflowed with burgundy leather-bound books, row after row of Peacio's history now awaiting us.

Belle shoved her dark locks over her shoulders as she

marched into the first row. "Everything is filed alphabetically, so we'll grab the tomes labeled "C" for Chaser and begin there," she instructed.

"How many tomes cover the Chasers?" I asked as I strode after her. The darkened recesses, lit only by the odd overhead light, cast shadows across the ancient volumes. I slowed and swept one finger along the spine of one incredibly chunky tome.

"Several from memory and each volume holds several hundred pages. In particular, we need to be on the alert for any possible mention of the *being* you saw in the stables." Belle found the tomes we needed and Sorrell held out his arms for her to stack them into.

At the front of the library, Sorrell set his arm-full on the large oak desk with its chunky carved legs and solid wooden chair polished to a high sheen. He tapped his head as he eyed me. "Asar is on his way. I asked him to drop by our parents' home and pick up our Sona family journals. We have a couple of volumes kept by our ancestors and we agreed they might be needed since they cover Chasers and Destroyers alike."

"That's a great idea." The more records we had to look through, the more chance we might have at discovering who or what the Darkness was.

"We're not going to stop until we uncover this monster." Belle gently squeezed my arm then settled herself in the desk chair and opened the first leather-bound book. Belle spent a great deal of time in these archives, maintaining the recordings and adding to them as new information came to hand. This was one of her favorite places to be.

The air swirled and Asar shimmered in wearing a billowy blue shirt and leather pants, two chunky journals in his hands and a few streaks of blond now showing through his midnight black hair. He handed one journal to Sorrell and said, "I snuck these out of the house. I thought that best rather than having to explain to our parents what was going on."

"We'll let them know what's happening once Goldie has informed her father." Sorrell sat on the long burgundy padded couch against the closest wall, his journal in his lap. "For now, the less people who know about Goldie's skill, the better."

"Agreed. You take the second journal." Asar passed the other across to me, then he pulled me into a gentle hug, which both surprised me and had me hugging him fiercely in return.

"Thanks for bringing these, Asar." I eased onto the couch next to Sorrell.

"Anything you need from me, just ask." Asar nodded and chose a tome from Belle's desk and settled himself in the corner wingchair.

Taking the utmost care with the aged Sona family journal, I carefully brushed away a trace of dust from the deep blue leather covering it and turned the first page of parchment within.

"Don't ever disappear on me again." Sorrell's breath fanned my cheek as he leaned closer. "Not like you did this morning. Where you go, I go."

"I'm an independent girl."

"I don't wish to change that about you, but you've got to make room for me now. The Darkness said he was coming for you, and I'm not letting him get anywhere near you." He nipped my ear, and I frowned at him. His sensual lips lifted and drat it all, I couldn't growl him like I wanted to when he showed his emotions so strongly with his smile.

"I'm not letting the Darkness get anywhere near you either." I touched a finger to his closest armband then to my identical one holding the same inscription.

"Start reading." He tapped the page I'd opened to. "We can argue some more later. We've got a lot to get through today."

We surely did.

I got to work and delved into the journal.

Destroyers had graced the Sona family line for centuries upon centuries, a long line of dedicated guardians watching over the Chasers they'd given their blood oaths to eliminate when they turned Dark. The earliest accounts were documented by two of their family members who hadn't wished to lose the information told down through the generations. I absorbed each and every recording the historians had noted, then came to the transition where family members who'd held the skill recorded their own dealings with their Chasers. Such a fascinating insight into the Sona family and their personal thoughts and actions as Destroyers.

Mesmerized, I barely noticed lunchtime passing other than for Silvie who dropped off sandwiches, fresh jelly donuts, and drinks. I licked my fingers as I polished off my lunch, then Sorrel and I switched journals not long afterward, and I got immersed in the second journal.

Belle and Asar were equally as engrossed in their tomes.

Near the end of the second journal, I came across a recording by Siovanni Sona, who'd been assigned to the last Chaser to ever grace our world, or at least the last until me. His name? Avil Saville, a Peacian.

I absorbed the information recorded, which detailed Avil's downward spiral and Siovanni's struggle to contain him. Siovanni—in order to contain the Chaser—had ended up drugging Avil in his sleep, then he'd locked Avil away deep within the Loveria Castle dungeons. Of the most interest though, was that Avil had never awoken from his drug-induced sleep and simply faded away over the next seven days. After he'd breathed his last in his cell—his body released to a close friend afterward—he'd been entombed within the Saville crypt.

Hmm, I itched to learn more about the last Chaser.

I set the journal aside and without interrupting the others, quietly wandered down the rows in search of the tomes which would cover the Saville family history. With that line being Peacian alone, it had never been covered with my country's tomes.

I searched the volumes under *S*, found the one I needed covering the Saville family line, and leaned against the rear wall.

Immersed, I read.

Two nights after the entombing of Avil Saville, noises from the family crypt had been heard by a clergyman walking past, but when the man had opened the crypt, he'd found only the wrappings which Avil had been covered in and no body. Red eyes had glowed from one shadowed corner within a hooded cloak then whatever it had been, dissolved into a black mist and swept out the door.

Holy moly.

I barely breathed.

The description sounded exactly like the *being* we'd seen.

I tapped the page and continued reading. The clergyman had alerted the authorities after securing the crypt once more, but with no further sightings ever made, all had been left alone.

Wow. Two hundred and twenty-five years had passed since Avil's entombing, and he'd definitely been sighted once more. By me, Sorrell, and Asar, right on Wincrest property.

Grasping the tome tight to my chest, I strode back to the others and at the edge of the room, cleared my throat. All three turned their gazes to me. "I have something."

"Show us." Belle cleared a spot on the desk and patted the polished surface.

"I believe Avil Saville is the Darkness." I opened the tome, set it where they could all easily see the passage. Quietness reigned as they read.

"You're right." With a gasp as she finished reading, Belle rocked back in her chair and eyed me. "Avil Saville is the Darkness. The description recorded here marks him as the entity we're after."

"I agree." Raking one hand through his shaggy golden locks, Sorrell muttered at me, "The Darkness also referred to you as being one born of dual blood. He wants you, is going to return for you. That can't happen."

"He'll return, and when he does, I intend on fighting him. He deserves to die." I wouldn't let anyone else get hurt when it was me he was after.

"I've already told you. You can't kill him. You have to follow the rules set out for your kind." Sorrell gripped my shoulder, his frustration flaring free.

"I agree with Sorrell," Belle added. "You can't take his life, Goldie. Doing so would place a death sentence over your own."

"Yet he's already dead." I flung my hands in the air. "I can't win either way."

"Hmm," Belle murmured, her face scrunching up. "Which broaches the question. How on earth do we kill the undead?"

I had no idea, but I had to uncover the answer. I had no other choice.

"I need to call a meeting of the leading eight and update them, immediately." Belle rose from her chair and pulled me into a fierce hug. "We'll need a plan going forward."

"It's fine. I understand. Tell them what you need to."

"I'll remain with my mate until we've sorted out that plan." Firm words from Sorrell, his hand still on my shoulder, his other sliding around my waist, his hold implacable as he glanced at his brother. "I need some time alone with my mate."

"Take as much time as you need." Asar narrowed his gaze on me. "My brother doesn't wish to let you go and I understand why. You are his match in every way."

"We're a terrible match."

"Yet you are still the only one I want." A mutter from Sorrell, who currently meant business with those words, his resolve unbending. I sensed it in the way he held his body and tightened his hold on me even further.

I wanted to argue, to make him understand that I'd never allow him near the danger coming for me, only he sent us streaming away through the dark.

The wind rushed by and I swung around and yelled at him over the blustery blast. "You don't get to keep pushing *your* way as the *only* way."

"Yes, I do."

"No, you—" We bumped down next to the corral under a darkening sky, the day having passed swiftly within the library. Night had already arrived, stars glittering above. I slid my sword free of its sheath and waved it in front of his nose. "Let's discuss this in the way of warriors, shall we?"

I'd battle him to get my point across.

"I can't raise my sword against you. Never again. So put yours away, right now."

"Not happening." I swung, and he jerked back a step, sucking his belly in and arching his back out. I missed him by a whisker.

Snapping his teeth together, he shot me a feral look. "Don't make me draw my blade on you, Goldwyn Wincrest."

"If you don't, you're going to get hurt." I sprang forward again and he whipped his blade free and caught my blow with a fierce glint in his eyes. He pushed back, then came at me, heaving his blade into mine with one hard strike after another, his vicious blows pushing me back farther across the gravelly yard.

I banged into the side of the stables, my back coming up hard against the white weatherboards as he trapped me ruthlessly in place.

"I'm done battling." He sheathed his blade, plucked mine from my hand and slid it away in my scabbard before seizing my hips and zipping us straight to my bedroom.

I fell back onto my mattress with a whoosh, my blond hair falling across my face.

I shoved my hair away as Sorrell heaved my feet into the air and yanked off my boots.

He tossed them with a clunk into the corner, tugged his own

boots off then crawled over me and flattened himself on top. "You can sleep in your clothes with your weapons close at hand. We both need to be prepared for Avil should he return."

"Which he stated emphatically, that he would." I tried to squirm free, but that wasn't happening.

"We'll be waiting for him when he does, and that includes both Asar and me." He captured my hands, pinned my wrists to the covers over my head, then ducked in and nipped my neck. "You're mine, all mine. Never his."

"You're supposed to be emotionless, Sorrell, but you've got more emotions simmering within you than anyone else I've ever met." Oooh, and he was now sucking on my neck and making my belly flutter. My stupid body arched into him for more of his exquisite touch.

"That's because you see past the surface layer of me, to the man I am underneath." He brushed kisses along my jaw, touched his lips to mine and my heart sped up to a frantic beat. He kissed me long and deep, his mouth devouring mine as if he were on a mission to infuse us ever closer together, and good grief, I was falling for him and the spell he weaved so effortlessly around me.

"Your heart"—another soul-deep kiss—"is acting up."

"That's your fault for kissing me." I tried to tug my hands free of his fierce hold, but gave up when I got nowhere. "You shouldn't have aligned our heartbeats."

"I didn't have a choice," he whispered as he licked my lower lip then sucked on it, his words ringing with stunning clarity, which I picked up easily along our bond. "Close your eyes and go to sleep, my mate. Maybe your heart will begin beating correctly again once you're resting."

"It'll beat correctly again if you leave." I looked deep into his eyes, the gray-blue depths lit with a mischievous glint. "Ugh, you're not going to go though, are you?"

"Nope, not when you hold the other half of my soul and I

hold yours." His voice got all husky, the impossibly long length of his eyelashes sweeping his cheeks. "I give you my word I'll always keep you safe from harm, that I'll protect you from Avil Saville and never allow you to turn and go Dark. I want to give you all that you desire, and to never live a day without you. My life would certainly be a living kind of hell if I ever lost you. I know that now, to the depths of my heart and soul." He kissed me, with an intensity that melted away my resistance.

I needed him too, just as deeply as he needed me, but with my future so uncertain, there wasn't a chance I wished to drag him into it. Against his lips, I murmured, "What am I going to do with you?"

"Kiss me until we both fall asleep." He lifted up a touch and flicked the senses on over the headboard and with one of my hands free, I snagged it around his neck and brought his mouth back to mine.

I got busy, doing exactly as he'd asked, kissing him until we both fell asleep.

Chapter 11

The next morning, I awoke to the sun streaming through the glass slider and I released a blissful sigh at my dream-free sleep. I rubbed my socked feet against Sorrell's socked feet, my mate lying half over top of me, one arm hooked around my waist and one leg over my legs. Several locks of his golden hair swept across his forehead, others curled around his ears and along his shoulders. I pushed my fingers into his hair and cupped the back of his head, my heart melting at his sweet and possessive need to keep me close during the night. "At some point in time," I whispered in his ear, "you've got to stop pinning me to this bed and let me up."

"I'm pinning you, so that should you move, I'll know the second you do." He yawned and patted his mouth. "Did you sleep well?" he mumbled around a second yawn.

"I did, but you appear exhausted. Is there a reason why?"

"I slept on and off. I couldn't rest properly when I was so worried you might awaken from a dream of foreboding."

"There weren't any, which is a good omen for the day to come. Go back to sleep if you like." I wriggled and tried to free myself, but he only tightened his hold on me even more. "C'mon. You've got to relent and let me up."

"I can't catch some winks if you're not here." A grumbling mutter in answer. "Wherever you go, I go. No exceptions."

"We can't stay joined together at the hip all day. I need to use the bathroom, and you are not coming in there with me. A girl needs privacy, and right now I need privacy. Move it, Sorrell Sona."

"I'll give you two minutes."

"No, you'll give me five." Good grief. Why was I negotiating the time required for a bathroom break? I gripped his shoulders and heaved, and when he finally rolled over, I bounded on top of him. Puffing madly, I gave him my sternest expression, only he lifted his lips in an amused grin. "Stop smiling at me like you're winning this fight."

"I am winning it." He fastened his hands on my hips and stared at my lips. "I had no idea I'd fall this hard for you, or this fast. But I have, and it feels incredible."

"You're not falling for me. That's all in your imagination." I pushed upright until I sat across his hips, then I wagged a finger at him. "We need to lay down some ground rules. Firstly, I am the boss around here. Secondly, whatever I say goes. Thirdly, I am a Wincrest, and Wincrests are damn tough. Avil Saville isn't going to take me down, not when I'm taking him down."

"I love how tough you are." He lifted his knees, knocked them into my back and sent me sprawling forward.

"Oomph." I landed against him, chest to chest and eye to eye. I flicked the switch for the senses and gritted my teeth. "You are impossible."

"Three and a half minutes. We'll split the time."

"Five minutes. They'll be no splitting of time." I rolled off him and hit the floor at a run.

"Four minutes." He dove and tackled me around the legs.

"Sorrell!" I fell and he rolled in underneath me, cushioning the blow as I landed on him and not the snowy white carpet underfoot. I gasped at how quickly he'd moved, then he whipped to his feet just as quickly and set me back on my feet.

"A word of warning, my mate." He tapped my nose. "I

never lose a fight."

"Well, you're losing this one." I 'ported, zipping through the dark with the greatest speed I could. Sure, he'd be able to follow my airstream, but I could outsmart him. All I needed was a water source to mask my 'porting scent.

I bumped down next to the familiar cluster of bush trees bordering the closest water source to our homestead, then I bounded into the watering hole which Hope always took care in keeping at its highest level.

A bellow from Sorrell as he arrived in a blast of wind.

I dove and went under.

He dove after me, his hand closing around my ankle as I kicked away, although all he captured was my sock since I 'ported again, this time with a swift jump to the river bank where Hope sent the water farther inland with her water skill during the controlled river releases.

Glorious fields of green lay spread out before me, the mighty river rippling in between and pulsing with life. Birds soared across the sky then swept low and skimmed the rushes either side of the river. Thousands of head of cattle grazed across the lush green fields, and Guy waved his Stetson as he rode high in his saddle along the bank.

I waved back, yelled, "How's everything going down here?"

"All in order, but it appears you're being followed." He motioned to the wind twisting near me. Only a few feet away, Sorrell appeared with a furious scowl on his face and I laughed and dove into the river. I went deep, his fingers grazing my toes a second time, but I punched forward and 'ported again.

My heart lifted, freedom pulsing through me as I reemerged within Matilde's stall, the mare's head touching her foal's head in a beautiful mother and newborn moment. Both appeared healthy, happy, and well.

The air stirred again and I caught a glimpse of Sorrell as I flashed away, this time though I made a short hop to my bedroom. I skipped into my bathroom, flicked the lock and bounded into the shower. I giggled as warm water sluiced down my jeans and pooled in the shower basin.

"Goldwyn Wincrest!" A feral thump on the door. "If you take any longer than five minutes," he growled, his voice muffled through the wood, "then I'm coming in and will haul you out of that shower."

"I need ten minutes now." Laughing, I washed my hair, the water pulsing against me. I scrubbed and cleaned myself, rinsed the suds away and once done, flicked the lever off and dumped my wet clothes in the corner laundry hamper. I wrapped myself in a plush white towel from the vanity cupboard, brushed my teeth and ran a comb through my damp hair, then with my weapons in hand, halted with one hand on the door handle. I didn't doubt that if I opened the bathroom door, Sorrell would be standing there in wait.

Not wanting to chance that, I flashed straight to my dressing room.

I donned my favorite tan leather pants, added a fitted black t-shirt, strapped on my weapons and slid the snake bands up and around my upper arms since I'd removed them during my shower. Coiled perfectly in place once more, I traced over each one. I loved these treasured heirlooms and wanted to keep them so badly, although I shouldn't. Hmm, Sorrell wouldn't take them back, even if I shoved them into his hands. Perhaps I'd keep them on for a little longer. Surely that wouldn't hurt.

With my usual firm determination in place, I wrenched the door open to one fiercely aggravated protector striding from wall to wall within my room. He'd changed too, his hair damp and his jeans riding low on his trim hips. His sleeveless tan shirt was unbuttoned to his navel and as he turned, the sides billowed out and I got a mouthwatering glimpse of his hard abs and heavily defined core. His silver snake bands glinted from around his muscled biceps, his steely gaze narrowed aggressively on me.

"I want," he snapped as he stormed toward me and halted in front, "to sleep in your bed every night and awaken with you every morning. We need to get married."

"Pardon?" My eyebrows soared into my hairline, and I definitely lost ten very necessary heartbeats. "No."

"Most mated pairs marry young, and there's no need for us to wait since there isn't any other for me, other than you."

"We are never getting hitched." I gripped the sides of his shirtfront and buttoned it up. "I'm a Chaser, remember? Short life span. Usually a gruesome death at the end. Then there is the unkillable evil thing chasing me. You should be running for the hills, not running toward me."

"You'd make the perfect wife. You're stroppy and fierce, exactly as I am." He dipped his head and swept me away with a soul-shattering kiss. "I need you, Goldie. I want you."

"We are not getting married."

"Not today, there isn't time." A firm nod, followed by an equally firm eyebrow lift. "Although I can manage tomorrow. Are you free?"

"Argh." I kissed him just to shut him up, then since it was glaringly obvious he was extremely adept at following my 'porting airstream, whether I masked it or not, I held onto him as I sent us winging through the dark directly to Dralion.

It was time to come clean with my father, and with all that had gone down recently, that clearly couldn't wait any longer.

We bumped down in the foyer of Donaldo's wing on the fourth floor of Wincrest Palace. Here, the ceiling rose twelve feet high, with ornate plaster scrollwork surrounding a magnificent chandelier dripping in fine crystal. A dozen high-backed chairs covered in black silk sat propped against the walls, chairs I'd scrambled over hundreds of times as a child as I'd played outside my father's study. I was home, and I'd brought my mate with me, a protector my father would detest. I didn't doubt that. He'd always hated all things Peacio.

"I take it this is Wincrest Palace?" Sorrell cast his gaze about the foyer. "Is it time to spill the beans to your father, the ruthless Donaldo Wincrest?"

"Yes, which I'm not looking forward to."

"Neither am I." Yet intrigue shimmered in his eyes. "How close are you two?"

"I'm his only daughter and I look strikingly like my mother."

"That wasn't an answer."

"My father is a firm yet fair ruler, has been incredibly overprotective of me over the years, but as I grew older he set that overprotectiveness aside and allowed me to choose my own path, to live my life as I needed to. He's never told me what I should or shouldn't be doing, but instead supported whatever path I chose to follow, the station being that ultimate path."

"Which is how you and Hope came to run Wincrest Station?"

"The station was gifted to Hope and I years ago, has always belonged to us, and in running it we've been able to provide for so many of our people here in Dralion. Come with me." No more dallying. I needed to get this visit over and done with. Breathing deep, I strode toward the two oak paneled doors, pushed them open and stood in the doorway as my father sat at his solid oak desk speaking to two warriors at attention in front of him, both men clothed in heavy combat gear. My heart thumped and my pulse rocketed.

Donaldo Wincrest could be a fearsome sight to behold, and this morning was no different. His violet eyes cut directly to me, moved over every inch of my face, then slid to Sorrell towering over me from behind. At least my mate wasn't wearing battle leathers, although it was impossible to miss the weapons he'd donned and how firm and fierce he held himself. My mate was a fighter through and through.

"Don't raise your weapon against my father." I leaned back against Sorrell's broad chest.

"I won't, provided he doesn't raise his weapon against me." He stroked one hand down my side and clasped my hip, his touch a complete claim which my father hadn't missed.

With his chin lifted, Father flicked a hand at the warriors who immediately shimmered and disappeared. He stood, his brown hair thick, and his dark beard well-trimmed. Since our people lived easily to one-hundred and twenty, never aging from our eighteenth year when we reached adulthood and came into our strength skills, my father appeared as youthful as ever, yet also every inch the fierce warrior king of Dralion that legend decreed he was. In his perfectly pressed white-collared shirt with silver chains looped from his shoulder to his top pocket, his long legs encased in black leather pants and his sword gleaming at his side, Father strode toward me.

I stepped away from Sorrell and Father embraced me in his firm forearm hold, the gold insignia rings on his thumbs glinting in the sunshine streaming through the large square windows. Beyond the panes of glass, the black granite cliffs of Dralion rose like an impenetrable force with the deep blue of The Great Orbiting Ocean rolling in and slapping hard against them. I cleared my throat. "Father, I'm sorry I haven't been home these past few days."

"You've been busy at the station. I understand that." My father eased back a touch but maintained his grip on my arms, his narrowed gaze once more on Sorrell. "You seem to have a shadow. Introduce me to the guest you've brought with you."

"Father, meet Sorrell Sona." I gestured with one sweeping hand to Sorrell. "This is a meeting I'd rather never happened, only it needs to, so we're both here."

"Sona?" Father's brows slashed down into a hard line, which was fairly impressive since they already had been. "The only family line of Sona within our world resides within Peacio."

"Ah, yes, that's right," I admitted. "Sorrell is a protector, the leader of his mountain team of protectors."

"I'm also mated to your daughter." Sorrell crossed his arms and planted his booted feet wide.

I gulped. "Unfortunately, that is also true."

"Tell me everything." Father's determined look brooked no argument.

"I've released him from our bond." That my father needed to know first and foremost.

"I haven't released your daughter." Sorrell chased my comment up fast. "Or I should say I did, but then I took that release back. I'll never release her again either."

Gah, I wanted to kick Sorrell.

I stepped between the two of them as they suddenly closed in on each other. Slapping a hand against both of their chests, I muttered, "Father, wait. I have news, and it's not about my mated bond with Sorrell. I've come to speak to you about something far more…awful."

"Nothing could be more awful than learning you're now mated to a protector. As it is, I have to put up with Faith being soul-bound to Davio Loveria, and Hope with Silas Carver. I will not," he hissed between the white lines of his mouth, "permit my own daughter to embark on a relationship with a protector from the Sona family. They're Destroyers, every single blasted one of them."

"You already know that about the Sona family?"

"I know everything about every Destroyer line gracing our world." He set a hand on my shoulder. "You can't remain with him, not when his kind are relentless. They're born and bred fighters who hold very few emotions."

"I don't want to remain with Sorrell, not when I'm a…ah…Chaser." I kept my gaze on my father and waited for that news to sink in.

"Pardon?" He jerked back as if I'd hit him, his violet eyes

going wide. "No, you're nineteen, a year past coming into your adult strength skills. You shouldn't be coming into any others. You can't be a Chaser."

"Goldie is what she states she is," Sorrell bit out. "Your daughter came to me, requesting I be her Destroyer and I agreed to her request, except we soon discovered our bond and have had to since employ a second Destroyer to her, my brother, Asar."

"We have Destroyers within Dralion, Goldwyn, the Furor family." Father's nostrils flared, his knuckles going white as he fisted the hilt of his sword. "You should have spoken to me first, then to one of them. Several members of the Furor family are warriors under my command and would be a far better choice of guardian than anyone from the Sona family line."

"If I had chosen a warrior Destroyer from Dralion then they might've hesitated in their actions with me."

"I would never allow any of the Furors to harm you."

"My point, exactly."

"Hold on, everyone, I'm coming in!" A shout from Faith in the foyer. Wearing sleek battle leathers, she skidded in, her blond hair flying and sword belted at her hip. She grasped the tiny bump of her belly, her breath whooshing out. "Wow, they love it when I move that fast, the little daredevils."

"Faith, you shouldn't be racing about like that." Donaldo gently pressed a hand over Faith's. "You're carrying my great-grandchildren and I won't have any harm coming to them."

"Grandfather, I had a vision of forewarning and bolted straight here." Faith reached up onto her toes and kissed Donaldo's cheek. "Although thank you for your concern."

"What did you see in your vision?" Father searched Faith's gaze, Faith holding the same revered forethought skill as Alexo.

"A brutal sword fight going down, between you and Sorrell, so keep your swords sheathed." She nabbed a dagger sitting on the corner of Donaldo's desk and shoved it into a drawer. "Right, that's one less weapon that might go flying about."

"I had the same vision." In an inky-black silk shirt and pressed dress pants, Alexo strode into the room and halted next to Faith and me. "The vision hit me hard and fast. I'm now aware Goldie is a Chaser and holds the assassin ability, as well as the fact that she's being hunted by Avil Saville, the last Chaser who can kill even though in spirit form."

"Oh yeah, I forgot to mention that part of the vision." Faith squeezed my hand. "I'm sorry about the Darkness, but none of us will ever let Avil take you from us, not now, not ever."

"No one hunts my daughter and lives." Father gritted his teeth as he eyed Alexo. "Tell me everything you saw, and don't miss a single detail out."

"Of course." A firm nod from Alexo, my brother a solid force, exactly as my father was. "Avil intends to return for Goldie. He believes she's of dual blood, although I'm unsure what that yet means. He appeared as a cloaked figure in my vision, his form little more than a black mist with glowing red eyes, although he did bring forth fingers, albeit blackened and nasty."

I stepped forward. "Father, I've seen Avil and he isn't human. He recently came to the station, and Sorrell and Asar fought him, although no strike against him brought him down. He simply transformed into a black mist and streamed away in his spirit form." A simplified version, but it would do.

"What else do you know about him?" Father gripped my chin, kept my gaze focused solely on him. "You're not telling me everything and I must know."

"Yesterday, I spent the day in the Loveria Castle library with the Belle Benner, Sorrell, and Asar. The four of us scoured through the tomes, as well as the Sona family journals which have been kept by Sorrell's ancestors throughout the centuries. Within one of those journals I learnt of Avil and the Destroyer assigned to him, Siovanni Sona. Avil spiraled downward quickly and Siovanni struggled to contain him, and in the end, he drugged Avil in his sleep before locking him away in the dungeons. Siovanni recorded that Avil never awoke from his drug-induced sleep and instead faded away over the next seven days. After he breathed his last, his body was released to a close friend, then entombed within the Saville crypt." I drew in a deep breath. "Two nights after his entombment, noises from the family crypt were heard by a clergyman walking past and when he opened the crypt, he found only the wrappings which Avil had been covered in and no body. Red eyes glowed from one shadowed corner within a hooded cloak, then that form dissolved into a black mist and swept out the door. Avil was the last Chaser, until I came into my skill."

"No, you're not the last, Goldie." With his fingers still firm on my chin, Father pressed a kiss to my forehead. "There have been others, two to be exact, both born in the last century and both having since perished."

My mouth gaped open. "Why have I never heard of them?"

"I gave them both my oath of protection, which meant I spoke to no one about them, not even to you or Alexo."

"How did they die? You said they perished in the last century."

"The first Chaser was William Iona, a man mated to a Destroyer."

"William Iona? As in my grandfather, my mother's father?" William Iona had died very young, at age nineteen, if I wasn't mistaken. That much I recalled from what I'd read about that side of my family.

"Yes, William was your mother's father."

"You said William was mated to a Destroyer." He'd been wed to Diadra, my grandmother, who I'd unfortunately never met, not when she'd passed away the year my mother had turned nineteen, only a year following my own parents' wedding. There had certainly never been any mention of Diadra being a Destroyer and I'd scoured our family records well.

"Allow me to explain from the beginning." Father drew in a deep breath, then slowly released it. "William was the only Chaser to have ever been born within his Iona family line, and he was a Chaser who never spoke of his skill either. He wed Diadra, his Destroyer mate, and even though William suffered from terrible dreams of foreboding, his wife was determined to ensure he never assassinated any of the killers he'd seen in his visions. Diadra even managed to cut William off from the chase each time he embarked on it, but he didn't survive more than a year after he came into his skill. He took his own life at nineteen, rather than having to force his own mate to destroy him. Although what William never knew at the time of his death, was that Diadra was carrying his child—your mother— the first among our people to be born with dual Chaser-Destroyer blood."

"My mother had dual blood?" Oh whoa. My mind spun, so many questions roaring through it. "How did Diadra come to be a Destroyer?"

"Diadra was adopted, which I discovered by chance. Her parents had never told her about that adoption. She'd always believed herself to be their natural born child."

"So many secrets." I fluttered a hand over my mouth. "Please, continue."

"I managed to trace back Diadra's true lineage to the Furor family. She never wished for anyone to learn of her destroyer ability, not when she had no desire to be a Destroyer, and even more so when she accepted the bond with William and discovered he was a Chaser. They both wished to keep the secrets of their skills to themselves, or that was until I discovered a mated bond forming between myself and their daughter, Vespera. At that point Diadra told me everything, and I agreed to keep her secret and William's since he'd been gone for so long. Your mother of course knew the truth, but we never spoke of it to another."

"You said the first Chaser was William Iona. Who was the

second?" My heart raced as Sorrell moved in behind me. He wrapped an arm around my waist and tucked me back more fully against his chest. "Father," I continued, "leave nothing out. It's imperative I hear it all."

"Your mother was born to Diadra eight months after William's death, and when Vespera came of age at eighteen, she too held the dreams of foreboding which a Chaser does."

"My mother was the second Chaser?"

"Yes, although she was far different to any other Chaser who'd ever come before her."

"In what way?" Faith asked as she stood side by side with me, Alexo behind her, his mouth agape and his shock clear to see.

"Vespera could never have harmed anyone, not even though she held the battle skill. She was a fierce warrior, make no mistake about that, as well as a wonderful and loving wife and mother, but never once did I have to hold her back from assassinating a killer she saw within her dreams of foreboding. She never crossed that line, or had any desire to, and I wholeheartedly believe that was due in full to her dual Chaser-Destroyer blood. She certainly restrained the killers she caught, but then she always delivered them immediately to my dungeons, where they were each dealt with accordingly. She sought justice in the correct manner and I vowed"—Father thumped his chest, his voice all raspy and rough and filled with intense emotion—"to always guard and watch over her. She was my wife and I loved her dearly. When I lost her, I was never the same. Her death hardened me, and I became far more ruthless in my dealings. I never told either you or Alexo about her assassin ability, because she never crossed that line and assassinated another."

"I see." Tears misted my gaze, my father's pain becoming my own. "You have never been ruthless with me, slightly overbearing, yes, but ruthless, no."

"You remind me so much of your mother." Father squeezed my fingers as he cast his gaze to my brother. "Alexo, I was most certainly ruthless with you. Two months after your mother's passing, you came of age and into your skills. You held forethought, could see visions of impending doom and you also disappeared time and time again. I feared you too held the Chaser ability as Vespera had, and I feared that you feared telling me. Only when I confronted you about your wanderings, you admitted to a mated bond taking form with an Earthling. An Earthling!" An aggravated rumble vibrated from Father's chest and escaped up his throat. "Naught could have enraged me more and I made threats and threw my weight around. I would have destroyed Kate had you brought her home at that time."

"I knew and understood that too." Alexo cleared his throat, emotion strong in his voice as he uttered, "You forced me to keep every move I made with Kate a secret. Even she had no idea I was from another world, yet every time I left her on Earth and returned to Dralion, you had me followed so closely. I couldn't even sneeze without a warrior reporting it to you. It wasn't an easy time, then Kate fell pregnant, and I couldn't have been more happier or more in fear. To ensure her survival though, I had to give her up, Faith as well. It killed me to leave my wife and daughter behind."

"You only left them because I forced you to abandon them, and unforgivably so, on the very day Kate gave birth to your daughters." Grief darkened Father's eyes as he cast his gaze to Faith. "Your sister was born with a heart defect and after her birth, she stopped breathing, which was why your father brought her home. He intended on burying her on Dralion soil, only the teleportation jump triggered her heart into beating again. Our healers watched over Hope day and night until we were certain she would survive, although your father never spoke of you, that the daughter he'd returned with had been born a twin. Since your return to our family fold though, I've wished only to apologize to you, your mother as well. I wronged you both and should have told you so well before now."

"At least you're explaining it all today." Faith's gaze softened, a tear streaking down her cheek. "Grandfather, you should have spoken of this sooner. My mother always taught me that when wronged, we must still offer forgiveness so we can move on. It's essential for our own wellbeing."

"Your mother is a very wise woman. And as we've learnt since her arrival here with you, she was never an Earthling at all, but the lost child of Nathwer Sol, the last tribal leader of No-Man's Land."

"I wish you'd explained yourself to us sooner too." Kate stood in the doorway with Hope, both silent and unmoving, Kate's arm around Hope's waist and a tissue in her hand.

"I'm a stubborn and obstinate man, Kate, and always will be." A profound admission from my father, and it tugged at my heart. "I apologize for all the hurt I've caused you and Faith over the years, Alexo and Hope too."

"You're forgiven." Kate crossed to him in her white blouse and slim navy skirt, kissed his cheek and smiled at him. "You're a tough old goat, but I can handle you."

A smile from Father. "I'm beyond glad that Alexo has finally brought you home. You already stand so strongly at my son's side, and seeing so brings immense happiness to my heart."

"Now you're just trying to butter me up." Kate grinned as she backed up a step into Alexo's arms, my brother wrapping his wife up close, Alexo's love for Kate so clear to see in his eyes.

Father cast his expectant gaze back over Faith and Hope. "Might I ask for the forgiveness of my granddaughters too?"

"Absolutely." Faith hugged Donaldo.

"I finally feel like my entire family is whole again." Hope sniffed and wrapped her arms around Donaldo, then stepped back with Faith until they stood at Alexo and Kate's sides. "Now though, we need to make certain we keep it whole."

"Agreed." Father clasped my shoulder. "Now I've learnt you hold your mother's dual blood, I can promise you that you're a new breed of Chaser, a breed which defies the last."

"Do you truly think I'll be as my mother was? That I'll be driven not to assassinate any killers I catch, but only to ensure they are locked away?"

"I've no doubt about it, particularly when you're so very much like her." Father cast his gaze to Sorrell, a very drilling gaze. "If I've learnt anything these past few months with the return of Faith and Kate to my family fold, then it's that I will do whatever it takes to keep my family whole and safe. Make no mistake, Sorrell Sona, if you ever harm my daughter, I'll kill you, but if you remain steadfast at her side, then we will get along just fine."

"I'm the only one who can never harm her." Sorrell rubbed his chin across the top of my head, his stance at my back unwavering. "Our mated bond could even be called divine intervention, what with it being the joining of another Chaser and Destroyer. Surely that will ensure any children we welcome into this world will bear even stronger dual blood. My brother and I will certainly guard and watch over your daughter for the rest of our lives."

"Yes, you're right about the increased strength of the dual blood within your future offspring. I hadn't considered that." Father gently touched my cheek with the back of his curled fingers. "You are my daughter and I will never allow anyone to hurt you. Capturing Avil Saville is imperative, and all of us in this room will aid you however we can. There must be a way to contain and restrain him, and we shall find it."

I wouldn't accept any other outcome either, not now I finally had a chance at a long life.

I'd never allow it to be cut short by the evil thing coming for me.

Chapter 12

In the Loveria Castle training hall, I grunted, hooked one foot out and snagged it around Sorrell's knees to bring him closer to me. He toppled forward, caught one arm around my waist and snarled as Asar gripped his arms from behind and wrenched him away from me. I lost him, and drat Silas and Davio, they now aided Asar in pinning my mate to the wall and keeping me from him. "I told you before, and I'll tell you again," I muttered under my breath as I stormed toward the men. "Don't take Sorrell away from me, or else I'll hurt you all."

"Taking him away from you is the whole reason behind this training exercise." Davio came at me, meeting my attack head-on as I thrust my blade at him.

Sorrell bucked and hauled free, then rammed his shoulder into Davio's back and sent the two of them sprawling across the floor. "You're fighting dirty," Sorrell bit out at Davio as he rolled and made a grab for me.

"Do you expect Avil to fight any less dirty when we finally find him and confront him?" Davio nabbed Sorrell's boots and hauled him back across the polished floorboards on his back.

Sorrell kicked and managed to free himself, then he bounded to his feet and met Silas and Asar head-on as they plowed forward. Their blades clashed. Not fair. There were three of them against the two of us, and my mate was short on weaponry.

I skirted around Davio, swiped another blade from the rack against one wall and with a whistle to alert Sorrell, tossed it to him.

A wink as he caught it then with a grin, he swung both blades against Silas and his brother.

"Come here, Wincrest." Davio chased me and I barely caught his next high strike right over my head. "Got you," he snapped in my face. "Show me your wild side. Go hard and don't hold back. Imagine I'm Avil Saville."

My arms shook as I tried to keep him from flattening me. This close to him, my Wincrest blood having always battled against his Loveria blood, I gritted my teeth and pushed back, but unfortunately only managed to gain one single inch. "I don't know how Faith puts up with you."

"He can be rather annoying," Faith yelled from the sidelines where she, Hope, Belle, and Nicolas watched on, Nicolas leaning casually against one wall. Faith edged closer, gave her ponytail a tug, her gaze focused on the fight and me. "If you need a hand, Goldie, I'm your girl. Shout out, and I'm there."

"You stay right where you are," Davio barked at Faith. "You're pregnant, or have you forgotten?"

"Our babies like it when I fight." Whipping her sword free, she bounced closer.

"They do not."

"Do too."

"Not." Davio glared at Faith.

"Too." She glared right back at him.

"Think outside the box, Goldie." Hope side-stepped along the sidelines. "You can do this. He's a Loveria. Take him down."

Yeah, I could take him down. Outside the box. I loosened my elbows, only a touch as I kept my sword firm in my hands, Faith's need to join us distracting Davio. Oh yeah, distraction. I'd distract him the very best way I could. I leaned in and kissed him, right on the mouth.

He growled, jumped back and swiped a hand over his lips. "Quit that, Wincrest."

"Oooh, now that's thinking outside the box." Hope clapped and beamed. "Davio and Goldie sitting in a tree. K-i-s-s-i-n—"

"You kissed my mate?" Sorrell shoved Asar and Silas back then heaved toward Davio with a fierce scowl.

"She kissed me." Davio ducked Sorrell's wild blow, the steel of his blade coming dangerously close to nicking his ear.

"Sorrell's fury just doubled, and it hit me hard," Belle called as she followed Faith, keeping her in her sight and out of the fight like the overprotective empath she could be.

Silas and Asar bolted toward Sorrell, and I ran and dove, slid on my side across the polished floorboards and knocked into Silas and Asar's legs, which sent them both flying. I shot up and leaped onto Sorrell's back, then clung to him like a bear to a tree, my arms around his neck and my legs hooked around his waist. "I'm right here, big fella. I've finally got you all to myself."

"Stay on my back," he muttered as he swung at Davio.

I nuzzled his neck, his spicy, leathery aroma surrounding me. Oh wow, I wouldn't mind taking a bite out of him right now.

"Anyone thirsty?" Silvie hollered from the doorway with a tray of drinks, red straws bobbing. "It's time for a break. I'm calling a halt to this training session right now."

Oooh, she was my savior. I definitely needed a break, and to carry through with that bite. Davio stepped away from our fight and I clamped my mouth over Sorrell's neck, right over his fiercely beating pulse and sucked madly.

"Princess." A husky growl from him as he swung me around from his back to his front, then with his hands under my tan leather-clad backside, he dipped his head and kissed me. I clung to him, kissing him just as ferociously back.

"I have food," Guy announced as he joined Silvie, a platter of toasted sandwiches— ham and cheese going by the delicious scent wafting toward me—in his hands.

"Pickles and dipping chocolate for anyone?" Silvie, waving a jar of pickles, lifted a knowing brow at Faith.

"Yes, me, me, me." Faith snatched the jar and dunked a pickle into the bowl of dipping chocolate. She smacked her lips together as she ate. "Mmm, sooo good. Sour and sweet together make an awesome combination. I love you to the moon and back, Silvie."

"I love you too." Silvie popped a kiss on Faith's cheek then crossed to Silas and Asar still lying on the floor, their chests heaving. "You boys look thirsty." She held out the tray of drinks. "Fresh water from the well."

Davio strode across to Faith and dipped in for a hungry kiss. "Not."

"Too," she mumbled against his lips.

I cracked up as they continued to fight and kiss.

"I'm glad that training session is done." With one last nip of my lips, Sorrell lowered my feet to the floor, then accepted a drink from Silvie and tipped the straw toward me.

"Thanks." I sipped, then thanked Guy too as he handed me a toasted sandwich.

"Let's not forget why we're all here." Hope bit into her sandwich, her drink in hand as she eased down onto the floor next to Silas. "At the station, we need to increase our guard at night. Avil attacked there first, which means it's the most likely place where he'll attack again. Organizing shifts to ensure that guard is maintained in place will be best."

"Davio and I will sleep at the station and take a shift. Assign us whatever time you'd like." Wagging a pickle dripping with chocolate, Faith added, "We'll nail Avil if he dares to show his face. No one messes with us and gets away with it."

"Guy and I will stay at the station too. Give us whatever time you'd like." Silvie raised her hands and brought fire flaring to life on her fingers, the flames a match in color to her bright red summer skirt and tank top. She bounced her fire from tip to tip then sent one long flare arching out. A burst of fiery red licked the top of Silas's hair. "I want to toast Avil with my fire. I can't wait to see him burn."

"Silvie!" Silas glared at her as he patted his head and doused the flame. "I'm not Avil, so stop trying to toast me, sis."

"I'm just practicing for when I do see him."

"I'll get that flame out." Hope dumped her drink over Silas's head and water sluiced down his face. She giggled and Silas pounced and tickled her, the two of them rolling across the floor.

I giggled too. I loved seeing my loved ones happy, even though the current situation was incredibly dire.

"Aww." A soft sigh from Belle as she smiled at Silas and Hope. "I'm feeling your love for each other, and I love it. It makes my empath heart go all mushy."

"I'm sure you're actually sensing my love for you." Nicolas swept a finger under Belle's chin and tipped her gaze to his, a white light glowing from his hand.

"Hey, I'm not hurt. No glowy healing hand needed."

"I'm just making sure you're okay." With a wicked smile, Nicolas's hand glowed even brighter. "You know I can't help but check you over from time to time."

"More like every hour on the hour." Belle poked him in the chest then lifted onto her toes and kissed him. "Except secretly, I actually love that you do."

"I knew it." With a whoop, he spun Belle around. "How about we discuss exactly how much, in private?"

"There's a training session underway."

"Nope, it's break time." Nicolas glanced at Hope. "Put Belle and I down for a shift as well. We can be at the homestead in an hour, so we'll take the first one."

"Sounds great." A wave from Hope.

Nicolas flashed away with Belle, so fast.

"I wouldn't mind speaking to you in private too." Davio caught Faith's hand and licked her fingertips.

"What are you doing?" She tugged her hand back. "You're stealing my pickle juice and chocolate splatters."

"I would never do any such thing." A grin from Davio, so smug.

"Liar."

Laughing, Davio pulled Faith into his arms and cast Sorrell and me a smiling look. "I truly do need to speak to my mate in private. We'll be at the station before sunset. I give you my word we will." He twirled Faith away, shimmering and disappearing with her.

Another giggle from Hope as Silas nabbed Asar's water glass and threatened to tip it over her. She waved one hand and the water within swirled and with another flick of her fingers, she sent the water flying to the ceiling. Drops sprayed everywhere, and Hope beamed as she got wet.

"I love watching you play with your element." Lifting the three rose charms dangling from the center of Hope's necklace, Silas wrapped his fingers around them then sent the air swirling as he 'ported away with her.

"It's clearly time for all of us to enjoy a short break." Guy wrapped his arms around Silvie and nodded at Sorrell and me. "We'll see you two at the station. We'll take the shift after Nicolas and Belle." The two flashed away.

"I'll catch up with you both later as well. I've got an errand to run, which should take me half an hour, an hour tops." Asar clapped Sorrell on the back before shimmering and disappearing.

"Ah, I think everyone has just deserted us." Not a soul remained in the training room, just Sorrell and me.

"Which is a good thing." He backed me up against the wall and hemmed me in. "Do you have something to say to me?"

"Hmm, like what?" I arched a brow and tried to look all innocent.

"You know exactly what." He captured my mouth with his and kissed me, heatedly and passionately, until my head swam and I could barely keep my feet under me. "I want you," he murmured against my lips, "to revoke your release of me. You're of dual Chaser-Destroyer blood, from a new line of Chasers that don't assassinate. You're mine, always mine."

"I guess I could revoke my release."

"Say the words." Another dizzying kiss. "Our bond grows stronger with each hour we are together. Marry me, Goldie."

"Not today, there isn't time." With a teasing grin, I played with the buttons of his tan shirt, his armbands glinting across his biceps. "I'm not sure tomorrow's good for me either since there's still a killer on the loose, but I definitely don't want you sneaking away from me and hooking up with any other girl, so I hereby revoke my release. You're mine, Sorrell Sona, no matter what our future brings."

"That's all I needed to hear." He seized my lips with his then sent us zipping away through the dark.

Stars blazed all about and I kept my lips on his until we bumped down in the mountains on a crunchy matting of fallen leaves and pine nettles, right next to the edge of the cliff where he'd first brought me after we'd met in his arena. I nipped his lips. "How come we're here?"

"When two are soul-bound, they are mated for life." He gestured through the dense line of the trees. "You and I are now mated for the rest of our lives and I wish to do a short rewind back to that first day we met. You ready?"

"I sure am."

"Come with me." Holding my hand, he led me along the trail weaving through the dense line of pines then halted next to the thick patch of grass where I'd collected a handful to take back to the station. This time he tore a handful free and after pocketing it, guided me through the trees.

We walked past his team's log-built barracks and cabins

scattered about the meadow then together, we bounded up the front steps of his own cabin, the *swish, swish* of water streaming down the river making me itch to return to it for another swim.

"Is there a particular reason for this rewind?" I stroked my thumb along the inside of his palm.

"To destroy your letter." Underneath the overhanging porch of wooden shingles, he opened the door and steered me through before closing it with a soft click. The curtains were drawn, a touch of light penetrating through the thin blue cloth, the darkness within his quarters warm and inviting. He crossed to his table where my envelope sat, plucked the piece of paper from within free then returning slowly to me—his gaze holding mine—he tore the letter into pieces and tossed it high. Bits of paper fluttered to the ground, his smile wide and his steely-gray eyes softening as he pulled me into his arms. "I've no doubt you'll make fair and careful decisions moving forward, but regardless, I'll be by your side the entire time."

"Since you've been impossible to get rid of so far, I believe you." I couldn't contain my smile, or the sheer happiness soaring through me. "Sorrell, there isn't anywhere else I want to be, other than with you."

"From this day forward, the outback will be my home." He picked up my hands and pressed my palms to his chest. "Our relationship will always be a journey as we uncover more about your dual Chaser-Destroyer blood, but it'll be a journey we undertake together. You hold my heart in your hands, Goldie, and I never want it back. I love you."

"I love you too." With more love than my heart could contain.

"Isn't. That. Sweet." Growly words, red eyes glowing within the darkened shadows.

I froze.

Chapter 13

Darkness swirled all about me, a chilling, thick mist that clogged my nose and mouth. I searched frantically within the icy cold of the cabin for my mate. "Sorrell?"

"I'm here." Except his voice came from so far away.

"We have something important to finish." I got yanked deeper into the mist, Avil muttering in my ear, his blackened fingers digging into my middle.

"*Hope!*" I screamed to her along our link. "*I'm at Sorrell's quarters and Avil is here. Hurry, bring the leading eight.*" I had no choice but to ask for their aid, not when Sorrell would never give up his fight, and currently I couldn't let him do that on his own.

"Let go of my mate." A bellow from Sorrell and the whispered word *"Duck"* shimmering through my mind. I scrunched inward, tucking my head in even as I clawed at the blackened fingers for release. A blade whistled over my head and churned the mist and for a mere moment I caught a pinprick of Sorrell through the abyss of Avil surrounding me.

"I need her blood if I'm to shed this form and become whole again." Avil's mist swarmed thicker, colder, icier, choking me.

"Why do you want me?" I gagged for breath.

"The sorceress, Madam Seger, has told me that to reverse

my death, I must take the life of the one who holds both Chaser and Destroyer blood. I would have had your mother's, except Vespera Iona lay beyond my reach in Dralion."

"The energy dome was in your way?" More clawing. More gagging.

"Yes, which remained over Dralion for forty blasted years. I couldn't penetrate it from my resting place here in Peacio. Now though, I've got what I desire and no more will I wait." The scrape of steel echoed, a sword now in Avil's blackened hand.

"Siovanni Sona didn't get his chance to finish you, but I will." Sorrell roared and I caught a wisp of him as he attacked. Steel ricocheted against steel and boomed all about.

Outside, a rush of wind slammed the cabin door open, the mist swirling as Davio and Silas rushed in, Guy, Nicolas, and Asar right behind them. The girls chased after. I tore at the icy tentacles within the mist, but it swelled back out and smothered me.

"No one can stop me now." A screeching bellow from Avil, his darkness completely engulfing me.

I got sucked backward into a tunnel of wind. Kicking and thrashing against his black darkness, I tried to free myself, only he sent us speeding through time and space. Thunder rumbled and lightning speared through the dark of his 'porting tunnel.

"Hold your breath." His red eyes glowed. "We need a water source to escape your mate and the leading eight."

"My mate will never cease chasing me, and neither will my friends." I spat in his face and the blackened depths of his mouth opened. An evil laugh boomed and I jerked from the hit of misty black as it spewed all about me.

We hit water, hard.

"*Goldie?*" Sorrell's fingers skimmed my ankle in the rush. "*I'm coming, love.*"

More darkness.

Endless darkness.

A whoosh and metal slammed against metal.

I hit the ground, face first and water splashed across the hard stone floor underneath my cheek.

The mist streamed free and glided toward one wall where a candle shone within an iron wall sconce. The candlelight flickered over tombs surrounding me and down a murky tunnel of stairs leading into the depths of more darkness. A burial chamber. I was in a cold and gloomy burial chamber.

"*Sorrell?*" Nothing. No answer. I must be contained within steel.

I 'ported, hit steel and stone and *thunked* back to the ground. Damn it. This crypt definitely had steel encased within the stone, the door in front of me made of thick steel and Avil waving a key in his hand with an ugly smirk on his face.

"One needs a key to get in and out. Even I do." The key disappeared within his darkened form.

I patted my side, my sword gone, my wrist daggers too. Gah, he'd taken them.

Weaponless, but not without my fighting spirit, I shoved to my feet. "I take it this is your resting place?"

"Yes, where all within my Saville family line have been buried over the centuries. Of course, my line died with me since every Saville to ever live were born Chasers." He glided around the crypt, his cloak blowing out and the misty blackness of him swirling.

"So, you said you needed my blood if you're to shed your current form?" Since I was here, I might as well get some answers out of him.

"Correct." He halted before an alter holding a waist-high column with a marble basin perched on top. A flick of a match and he lit the oil within the basin. It caught alight, the flare of fire glowing bright.

"Well, you're not getting it, no matter what you want. I'm not on side with the whole dying thing." I side-stepped to the door, patted its cold surface. From top to bottom it stood without a crack around the edges. I kicked the door, muttered, "This place really sucks."

"It grows on one." He waved one hand over the fiery flames, the embers singing his blackened fingers and blackening them further. "The oil within this basin has been spelled by Madam Seger and now awaits your blood to be mixed with it. Once that's done, the flames will no longer burn me, but restore me."

"In my dream, you came after Saunder. Why the child?"

"You were late coming into your skill and I had to make certain your assassin ability had fully arisen. The child was expendable, although you altered the future by sending the child away. That's why I struck out against your mate and his brother instead."

"You're nothing more than a murderer, and I'm damn glad I'm nothing like you."

"Yet you still hold Chaser blood, the same as I do. Death sentences were handed down to our kind from the moment we stepped even one foot out of line." He lifted a dagger from within his cloak and plunged the blade into the flames. "It's time for your blood to be spilt."

A wind rose and howled, the drowning shriek echoing off the high ceiling. I nabbed a spike of wood gathering dust in one corner, only it was thin and brittle and useless. Still, I held onto it as he glided closer. *I'm sorry, Sorrell.* Even though he couldn't hear me through the steel, I would fight for my last breath. Wincrests never went down easily. *Forgive me for leaving you.*

More wind, it battered the crypt, then the steel door slammed open and Sorrell filled my vision, Asar at his side and the leading eight amassed behind him and his brother. *I'm here, Princess.*

A roar from Avil and blackness streamed around me, heat

singeing my neck. I heaved to the side, which sent the searing length of Avil's dagger sinking deep into my shoulder.

"Let me burn him!" Silvie bellowed and fire roared through the chamber as Sorrell and Asar ducked Silvie's fire as they dived inside. Flames licked at Avil's blackness, Silvie's red-gold hair and upper body completely ablaze.

"You're not having my mate." Sorrell hit me, and we rolled into the column. The marble basin smashed into the wall and Sorrell swung me onto his back as he heaved to his feet. I clung to him as Silvie's fire crackled. He slashed at the blackness, Asar at his side and Davio and Silas bounding into the fight across from us, their swords in hand.

Silvie's fire bubbled into a raging inferno, her flames engulfing Avil.

"With this spell," Guy yelled as he lifted his hands upward, his ability to enchant set free. "I hereby summon Silvie's fire. Within this chamber of stone and steel, all will cement and seal. All blood and bone belonging to the line of Saville, shall fuse together, and never once more be revealed." Two streams of pure white light poured from Guy's hands and arced over Avil encased in Silvie's fire.

The ground shook and the ceiling cracked.

Shards of stone smashed into the ground.

Sorrell swung me around from his back to his front then holding me to him, bolted out the door, the others racing after us.

The burial chamber crashed, steel melting and pouring inward with a last surge of Silvie's fire.

Faith, Hope, and Belle smothered me in Sorrell's arms, then Sorrell lowered me to the leaf strewn ground of the graveyard as Nicolas hovered his glowing hands over my shoulder.

"The wound is deep, but clean. I'll have no issue healing and sealing this." More glowy hands from my warrior healer and heat penetrated deep, the wound closing over right before my eyes.

"Goldie, are you all right?" Davio knelt at Sorrell's side, while over his shoulder the smoking ruins of the crypt were encapsulated with fiery-red steel, Avil's darkness entombed within.

"I am, provided he can't get back out again. Make sure of it," I demanded.

"We have." A firm nod from Davio. "Silvie burnt him to a crisp before the crypt fell. There was nothing left of Avil."

"Davio's right." Silvie blew out her fingers and sent me a wink. "Our enemy is toast."

"I love you, Silvie." I grinned at her.

"Aww, everyone loves me." A beaming grin in return.

"You are incredibly loveable, with a wicked skill." Faith bounced across to Silvie and hugged her, the wind whistling through and rippling the grass around the gravestones.

"It's the best skill ever." Hope joined Faith and Silvie in their hug, a huge smile on her face.

"I can't believe we did it." Belle squealed as she hugged the other girls too.

"The unkillable is now dead." Sorrell ran one finger along the pink line across my shoulder. "How are you feeling? Be honest with me."

"I feel like the luckiest girl in the world. You're the best mate I could've ever asked for." My shoulder loosened, the ache dispersing and as it did, I hooked my arms around Sorrell's neck and drew his mouth down to mine. I kissed him, with all the love I held in my heart, and a whole lot more. "I'm going to keep you."

"I'm keeping you too." Growling under his breath, he lifted me from the grass and holding me in his arms, the wind blowing his blond locks about, he arched a brow. "I think we've also managed to clear the schedule for tomorrow. Are you free to get hitched?"

"Definitely." My heart expanded, barely containing the love

I held for him within it.

"Then consider yourself engaged." He captured my mouth with his and kissed me, with a passion that made my head spin.

Cheers abounded, and we got smothered in hugs.

Giggling, I kissed him back and tasted his sweet love. I would hold that love close for a lifetime.

Chapter 14

Brimming with excitement, I rolled into bed that night in my favorite white nightshirt with gold stars all over it. "I can't believe we're getting married tomorrow."

"The priest is all organized." Seated in my corner padded chair, Sorrell leaned forward, his feet bare and hair damp from his shower, his elbows on his jean-clad legs.

"Why are you sitting over there?" I patted the space beside me.

"If I join you in your bed, I'll have my hands all over you."

"I like it when you put your hands on me."

"I should stay here." A frown as he slumped back.

"As you wish." I plumped my pillow and settled my head on it, a dreamy smile on my face as I rolled to my side and bumped into him. He'd 'ported fast, and I giggled. "I can always rely on you to be right here beside me."

"I need to kiss you again." He captured my mouth, his lips warm and full, his kiss wickedly delicious.

"We might have to have two weddings," I murmured as I dug my fingers into his arms, right over his silver snake bands. "My father isn't going to allow us to get away with a simple ceremony here in the outback. Can you handle a grand wedding at Wincrest Palace once all the plans are made?"

"I can handle anything your father throws at us."

"Good, then we need to check out the weather forecast for tomorrow."

"Huh?"

"For our honeymoon, which is beginning then." I rolled on top of him, pinning him to the mattress. "I want to go somewhere where it's pouring with rain. Lots of rain. An absolute downpour."

"I see." He chuckled, his lips on my neck as he sucked my skin. "I love you, and I can't wait for our lives together to begin."

"There'll always be a station to run, and it's a big one."

"I can handle the switch from the mountains of Peacio to the outback of Australia." He stroked over my armbands. "Provided I'm with you."

"How did you know where I'd be, during your chase of me?" I hadn't asked him that question yet, and I burned with curiosity. "I mean the Saville family crypt? I couldn't reach you through the steel and stone."

"Do you recall Avil's last words before he took you away from me? About the energy dome over Dralion?" Another nip to my neck.

"Yes, he said he couldn't penetrate the dome from his resting place, while he'd been trying to get to my mother."

"Exactly, *his* resting place."

"Oh, I see." I tapped his nose.

"Yes, but that wasn't the only clue that led me to you. After I lost you in his bid to use a water source to get you away from me, my heart told me where I'd find you. Everything within me got pulled toward the graveyard, and when I finally arrived there with the leading eight, it was clear to see the crypt had been constructed of stone and steel. You couldn't reach me because you were inside with Avil, and I couldn't reach you unless I tore that door down. Thankfully, Guy blasted it open with an "unlocking" spell, then the rest you know." He closed his mouth over mine, his kiss heating my blood and making my heartbeat pound.

Oh my. I loved his kisses, and I loved him, with all my heart.

I pulled back an inch and looked deep into his eyes. "Do you feel up to another chase with me?"

"Only if it's within this room." He took my face between his hands and kissed me again, exactly as I longed for.

Such a beautiful kiss.

With a lifetime of beautiful kisses and chases to come.

I didn't doubt it.

I would hold onto him until the end of time.

Never would I let my Destroyer go. Never again.

CHASER

Princesses of Myth

Protector, Book One
Warrior, Book Two
Hunter (Short Story - Included in Warrior, Book Two)
Enchanter, Book Three
Healer, Book Four
Chaser, Book Five

The Matheson Brothers

Highlander's Desire, Book One
Highlander's Passion, Book Two
Highlander's Seduction, Book Three

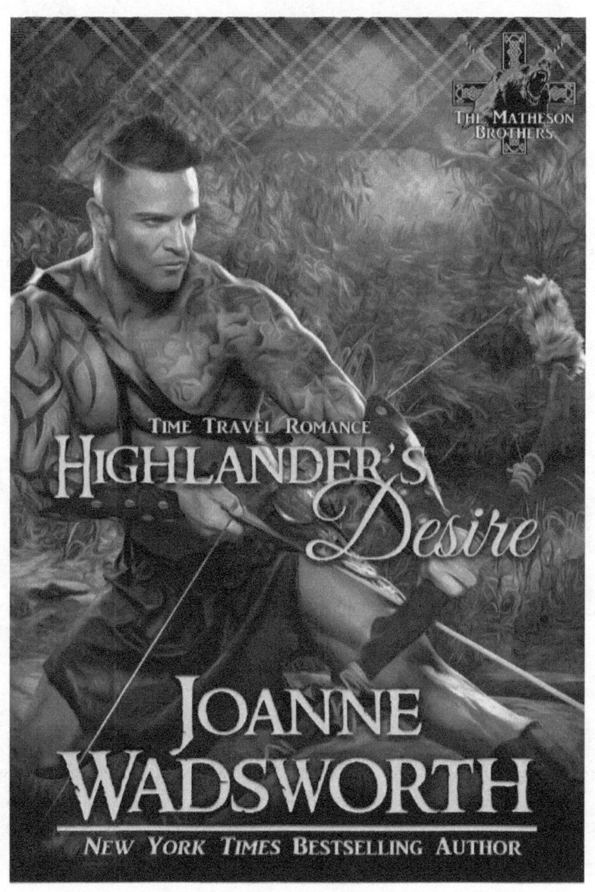

The Matheson Brothers Continued

Highlander's Bride, Book Seven
Highlander's Caress, Book Eight
Highlander's Touch, Book Nine

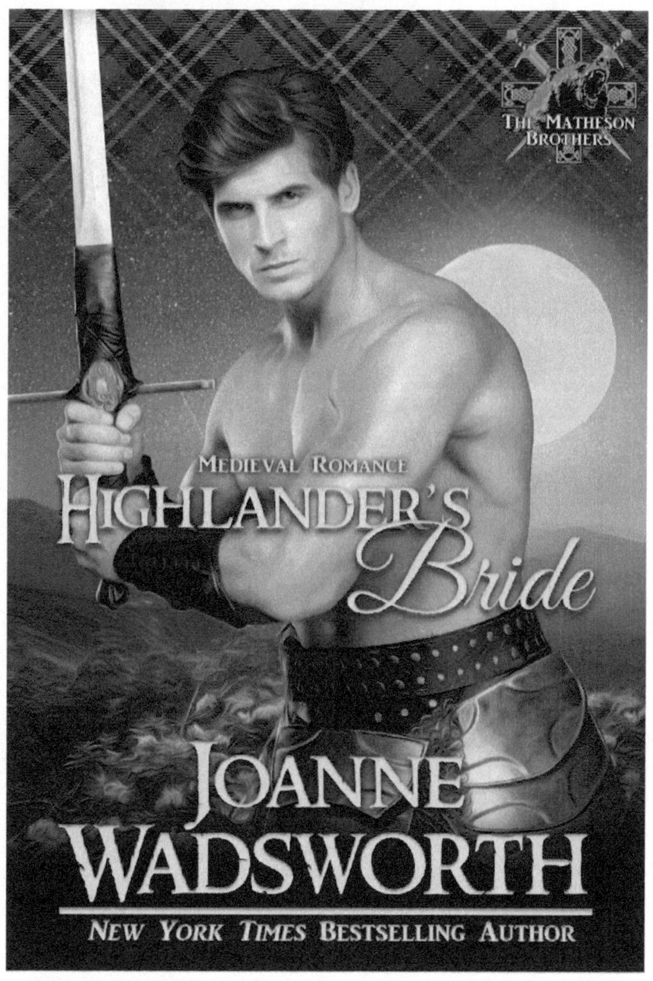

The Matheson Brothers Continued

Highlander's Shifter, Book Ten
Highlander's Claim, Book Eleven
Highlander's Courage, Book Twelve
Highlander's Mermaid, Book Thirteen

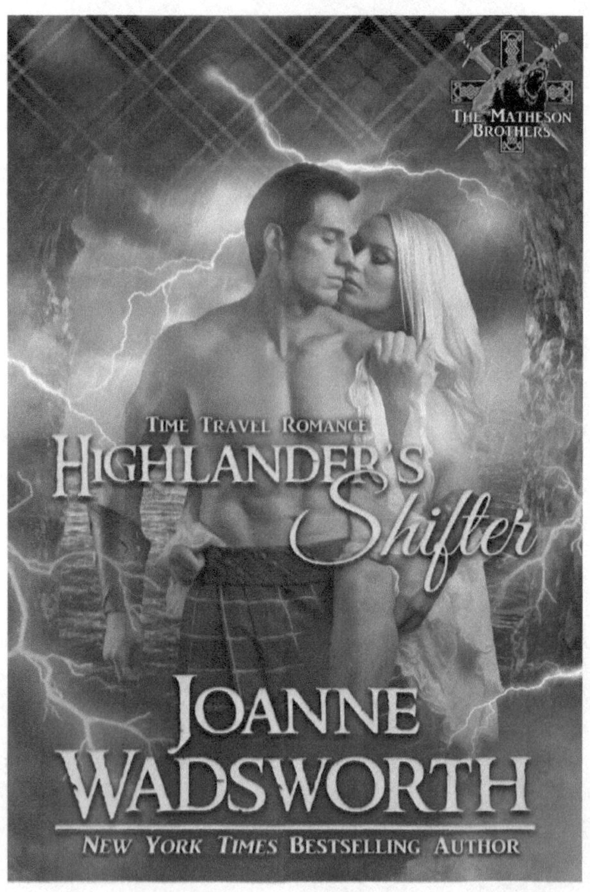

Highlander Heat

Highlander's Castle, Book One
Highlander's Magic, Book Two
Highlander's Charm, Book Three
Highlander's Guardian, Book Four
Highlander's Faerie, Book Five
Highlander's Champion, Book Six

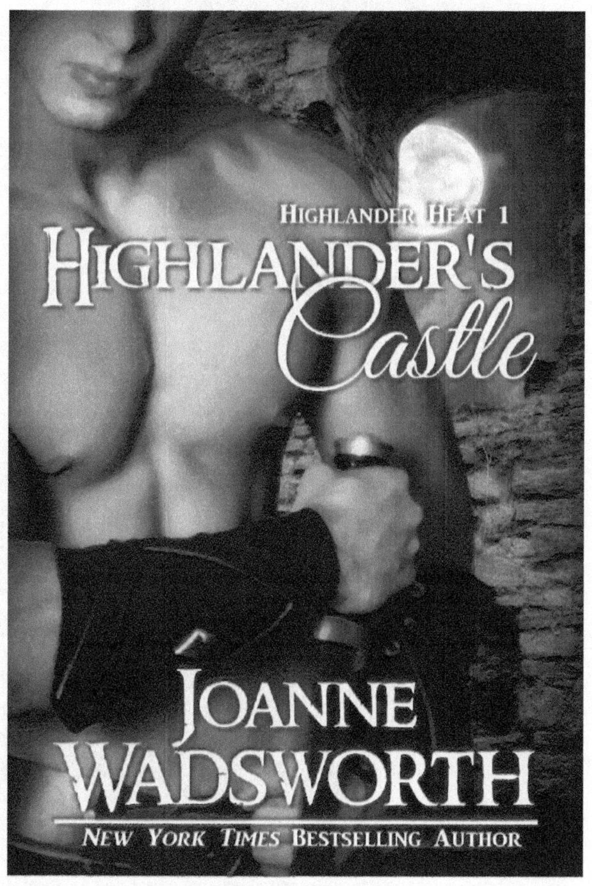

Regency Brides

The Duke's Bride, Book One
The Earl's Bride, Book Two
The Wartime Bride, Book Three
The Earl's Secret Bride, Book Four
The Prince's Bride, Book Five

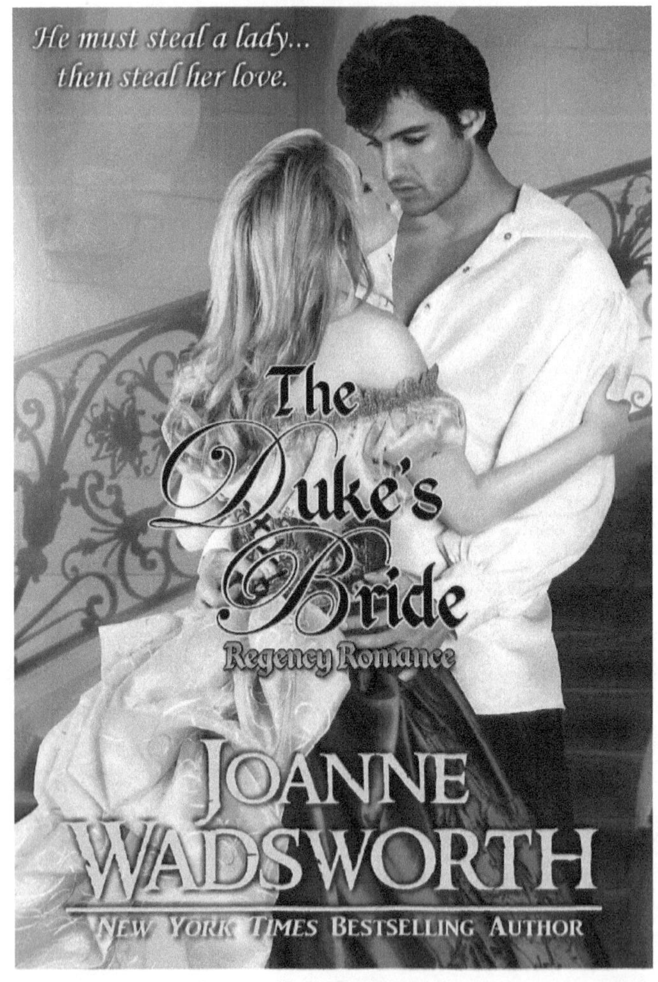

Billionaire Bodyguards

Billionaire Bodyguard Attraction, Book One
Billionaire Bodyguard Boss, Book Two
Billionaire Bodyguard Fling, Book Three

JOANNE WADSWORTH

Joanne Wadsworth is a *New York Times* and *USA Today* Bestselling Author who adores getting lost in the world of romance, no matter what era in time that might be. Hot alpha Highlanders hound her, demanding their stories are told and she's devoted to ensuring they meet their match, whether that be with a feisty lass from the present or far in the past.

Living on a tiny island at the bottom of the world, she calls New Zealand home. Big-dreamer, hoarder of chocolate, and addicted to juicy watermelons since the age of five, she chases after her four energetic children and has her own hunky hubby on the side.

So come and join in all the fun, because this kiwi girl promises to give you her "Hot-Highlander" oath, to bring you a heart-pounding, sexy adventure from the moment you turn the first page. This is where romance meets fantasy and adventure…

To learn more about Joanne and her works, visit
http://www.joannewadsworth.com